White Water

White Water

LINDA I. SHANDS

Fleming H. Revell
A Division of Baker Book House Co
Grand Rapids, Michigan 49516

Published by Fleming H. Revell
a division of Baker Book House Company
P.O. Box 6287, Grand Rapids, MI 49516-6287

Printed in the United States of America

Library of Congress Cataloging-in-Publication Data

Shands, Linda I., 1944-
    White water / Linda I. Shands.
        p.   cm. —(Wakara of Eagle Lodge ; 3)
    Summary: Fifteen-year-old Kara continues to experience hard work, danger, and excitement in the Oregon outdoors, and the exploration of her family's past, as she tries to use the wisdom God gave her.
    ISBN 0-8007-5772-6
    [1. Single-parent families—Fiction. 2. Christian life—Fiction. 3. Ranch life—Oregon—Fiction. 4. Oregon—Fiction.] I. Title.

PZ7.S52828 Wh 2001
[Fic]—dc21   2001031832

For current information about all releases from Baker Book House, visit our web site:

http://www.bakerbooks.com

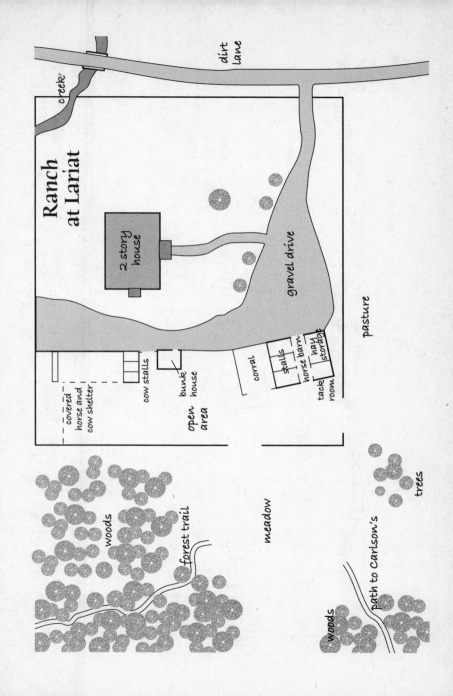

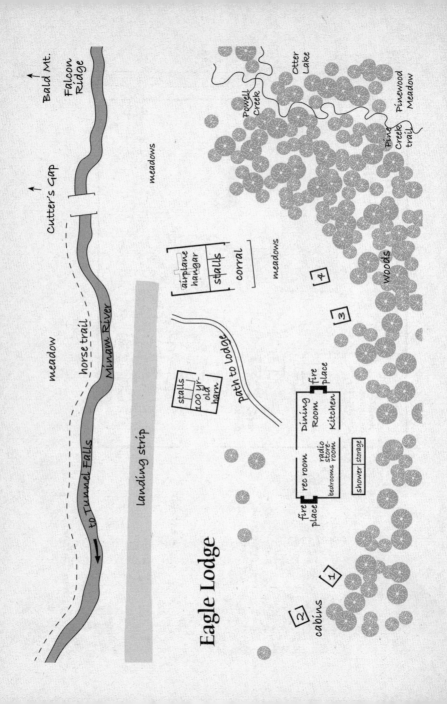

1

KARA FELT THE WHOOSH DEEP in her stomach as the plane swooped down between the canyon walls. It wound dizzily along, just a few feet above the twisting river, until a red-rock formation seemed to spring up right in front of them, then the right wing dipped and the plane soared high into the clean, blue sky.

In the blink of an eye, they were on the river in a wooden boat, rushing heedlessly toward a stretch of churning white water. The first dip made Kara's stomach leap again. She gripped the armrests on either side of her seat and hung on as the boat made a second, deeper plunge. Next to her, her seven-year-old brother, Ryan, squealed. Before she could turn her head to see if he was all right, the boat rose up and spun on a giant wave, then crashed once again into the raging water.

Kara realized she was holding her breath and let it out as the camera panned to calmer waters, then to a sandy beach.

She was fifteen, already a high school junior, and this had to be one of the most exciting films she'd ever seen.

The narrator's voice picked up the story of rock formations, wildlife, and daring explorations of the mighty Colorado River.

"Wakara?" She felt a tug on her sleeve and turned to catch Ryan's grin.

"What?" she whispered, hoping it would encourage him to do the same. It didn't.

"That was way cool!" His voice rose with excitement. "Will they show that part again?"

A few people around them chuckled, and Dad leaned across her with his finger to his lips.

"Not right now," she whispered back to him, using the same gesture as Dad. "Just be still and watch."

But Kara found it hard to concentrate on the rest of the film. She didn't know what was more exciting—this last-minute trip to the Grand Canyon, or the fact that in just a few hours they would be at Aunt Peg's in Phoenix to visit her and Grandpa Sheridan. Kara still couldn't believe it.

Grandpa had arrived from Ireland last November. He had visited with them in Lariat for a few weeks, then headed to Aunt Peg's in Phoenix, where he had been ever since. "I've had enough of the rain and cold," he'd told Dad. "I need some sun to thaw my bones. If it's all the same to you, I'll bask in Arizona for a bit."

Aunt Peg had called a few weeks ago and invited them all to come south for a few days. Dad had jumped at the idea. "We'll fly down next weekend," he'd said. "The kids have Friday off. School's closed for teacher training." Later he'd decided they could skip Thursday too and visit the Grand Canyon on the way.

Kara shook off her thoughts and turned her attention back to the seven-story movie screen. It was the first time

8

she'd been in one of the new IMAX theaters, and it was completely awesome. They had visited the Grand Canyon this morning and had taken the shuttle all along the west rim. The view had been sensational. But watching the video afterwards, she felt as if she were really soaring with the eagle, then gliding in an ultralight over the cliffs and the river below.

When the movie ended, she sat for a minute more, entranced, then followed Dad and Ryan to the gift shop, where they stood in line to buy a copy of the film. "It won't be the same on the TV screen," Dad said, "but at least the others will get some idea of what we saw."

Ryan ran ahead of them to the parking lot, then stopped and took Kara's hand. "That was so cool!" he beamed up at her. "Wait 'til Greg and Colin hear." His grin faded, and he slipped his other hand in Dad's. "I wish they could've come."

Dad's eyes clouded, but then he smiled and ruffled Ryan's hair. "Me too, Tiger. But your brother wasn't up to it, and Colin had to stay behind to take care of the stock."

All the way to the car, Ryan chattered about going to Aunt Peg's and seeing Grandpa. Kara tuned him out. She missed Greg and Colin too. It still didn't seem right having the family split apart on a trip like this. Mom wouldn't have stood for it. But Mom wasn't here, and Greg was still suffering the effects of a skull fracture he'd sustained when his horse went over a cliff last October during an early blizzard.

Kara sighed. Anne, their Nez Perce cook, would take care of him. And Colin was there to help with anything they needed. She felt a slight flush at the thought of Colin. He'd hired on as a ranch hand last June and was already part of the family. But she definitely did not think of him as a brother.

9

"Penny for your thoughts, Wakara." She looked up to see Dad holding the door of the rental car for her, a teasing grin flashing across his face.

Kara felt the heat spread from her hair roots to her toenails. "Uh, I was just thinking about how much fun this is!" Her voice sounded panicky. *Way to go, Wako.* She ducked her head and eased into the backseat with Ryan. Dad let it go and climbed into the driver's seat.

At the miniscule airport, they returned the car and climbed back into Dad's Cessna. Ryan slept on the short hop from Page to the airport in Phoenix. By the time they got clearance to land, Kara was yawning as well. But then they were in the passenger lounge, greeting Aunt Peg and Grandpa Sheridan, and Kara's tiredness vanished.

"Well, now, Wakara darlin', let me look at you!" Grandpa Sheridan's accent was thick as Irish cream, but Kara knew it was phony. She grinned and returned his bear hug, then stepped back as he held her shoulders and studied her face. "Sure, and it's me own mother's face I'm seeing here." His smile grew wistful. "You look just like her, Wakara, just like I remember her, and that's been a hundred years, or so it seems."

He had said the same thing back in November, still, Kara felt a glow of pleasure at her grandfather's words. She was proud of her Native American heritage. From the drawing she had of her great-grandmother, Kara knew she had been a beautiful young woman. And even though she had died when Grandpa was only five, it made Kara feel good to know he still remembered his mother.

Aunt Peg lived in a retirement community just outside of Phoenix. Her small, adobe-style bungalow would have fit snugly into the downstairs part of their ranch house in Lariat. Kara carried her suitcase into the closet-sized bedroom she would share with Ryan. Dad would bunk in with Grandpa.

Kara was secretly glad they were staying only a few days. The walled community teamed with people and cars, and even included a busy shopping center. Around the outside walls the desert spread dry and barren in three directions, while on the other side a four-lane highway separated the compound from the bustling city of Phoenix.

Between Ryan's tossing and turning and the roar of traffic, Kara was awake most of the first night. She drifted off to sleep around 2 A.M. and awoke to the delicious aromas of coffee, roasting turkey, and hot apple pie. Ryan's side of the bed was empty. She showered quickly, pulled on shorts and a T-shirt, and hurried downstairs.

"Whoa, that smells good, Aunt Peg. Need some help?"

Her father's sister beamed as she set the apple pie next to the pumpkin pies on the countertop to cool, then turned and held out her arms. "Oh, Wakara. Come give us a hug. I can't believe it's been over a year. Your mother would have our hides, God bless her."

Kara agreed, but didn't say anything. When Mom was alive, she made sure the entire family got together at least once a year. All except for Grandpa Sheridan, of course. Grandma Sheridan had died before Kara was born, and Grandpa had moved to Ireland shortly after. Still, Mom had always done her best to keep the family close.

Kara wrapped her arms around the older woman's slender shoulders and kissed her on the cheek. Aunt Peg's skin was brown from the sun, but still smooth, and she smelled like apple blossoms.

Her aunt returned the hug with a firm squeeze. Aunt Peg might be ten years older than Dad, but she was far from old in body and spirit.

"I accept the blame," Aunt Peg continued. "Your dad did invite me at Thanksgiving and Christmas, but there was just too much to do, and your grandfather kept insisting he

11

wanted sun, sun, sun. I don't know why, when he's spent most of the last five months with his head buried in that old trunk in the garage."

What old trunk?

Before Kara could ask, Aunt Peg said, "Sit and I'll pour you some coffee." She pointed Kara toward a chair and reached to grab a mug from one of the open shelves above the gleaming, white stove. Everything in the modern kitchen was either black or a sterile, gleaming white.

It's so clean, Mom would say we could eat off the floor. Kara giggled, and Aunt Peg flashed her a questioning look.

She started to explain, but a bloodcurdling scream echoed through the room.

"What on earth?" Aunt Peg clutched her chest and nearly dropped the coffeepot. Kara froze, then jumped up and sprinted out the back door.

"Ryan! What's wrong?"

Her little brother stood at the edge of the concrete patio, yelling, jumping up and down, and clutching his right hand as if he were trying to keep it from flying away.

She took hold of his wrist with one hand and grasped his shoulder with the other. "Hold still and let me see!"

"Oweee! It hurts, Kara!" he screamed. "Get it off, it's sticking me!"

"Wakara! What's going on?" Dad ran up behind her, while Grandpa and Aunt Peg closed in from the other side.

"I'm trying to find out." She tugged his hand harder, "Ryan, did something bite you? Let go and let me see!" Her heart pounded as she thought about black widow spiders, scorpions, and rattlesnakes—here in Arizona it could be any of the above, and they were all poisonous.

Aunt Peg saw it first. "Good grief, he's gotten into a saguaro."

12

"A what?" Kara looked closer. Sure enough, Ryan's palm was plastered with dozens of tiny splinters. "Oh, Ry, your hand looks like a pin cushion."

He started howling again, and Kara could have bitten her tongue. She looked up at Dad. "Sorry! Looks like he grabbed a cactus."

"I'll get the tweezers." Aunt Peg hurried back into the house.

Dad bent down to Ryan's level and took his hand. "Wow, I bet that smarts. Come on, let's get you inside and get these things out."

Ryan sniffed as Dad picked him up and turned to follow Aunt Peg. "I just wanted to pick one flower," he moaned.

Grandpa Sheridan chuckled. "Well now, lad, some flowers are for picking, but some flowers are best left alone." He patted Ryan's leg as Dad stepped past, then nodded at Kara. "I'm thinking he's just beginning to learn the difference, eh, Wakara?"

Kara started to ask what he meant, but she was interrupted by another scream from Ryan.

Grandpa winced. "Our Peggy will be pulling out the thorns. I think I'll take a little walk."

Kara watched him stroll around the side of the house and heard the latch rattle on the wrought-iron gate. She hesitated. A walk did sound good. Better yet, a nice long canter on her mare, Lily, across the meadow just behind the barn back in Lariat, or on the forest trail.

The smell of turkey drifting from the open kitchen window reminded her that there were still a thousand things that needed to be done for dinner. Aunt Peg wanted to celebrate all the holidays they had missed being together. Kara had thought it would be cool to celebrate Thanksgiving, Christmas, and Easter all at once, and it was—but it was also going to be a lot of work.

13

She sighed and looked back at the nearby giant saguaro cactus. A flash of white against the red-rock landscape caught Kara's eye. She bent down and studied the large, white blossom. It was beautiful. So was the desert, if you looked closely enough. And Aunt Peg's house might be ultramodern, but Kara had to admit it did look nice, and the tile floors were comfortably cool as well as pretty. She inhaled the warm, clean air, then picked up the flower Ryan had dropped and carried it into the house.

2

"Thank You, Lord," Dad prayed, "for all You have done for us." He went on to list the amazing ways God had provided for them in the year and a half since Mom died, and Kara found herself silently echoing his praise. A few months ago, she would have had a hard time finding anything to be thankful for, but now she realized that even though Mom had died, God was still concerned about the ones left behind.

God had brought Anne and Colin into their lives and had saved them, as well as her and Ryan, from a forest fire. God had also helped her to find Dad and Greg when they were trapped in a blizzard.

"And most of all, Father, we thank You that Greg is healing, and ask You to be with him and our other loved ones today. Amen." Dad's voice broke a little on the last sentence. When they raised their heads, Kara noticed everyone's eyes were bright with tears—as were her own.

Dinner tasted fantastic. Kara polished off a plate of turkey, mashed potatoes and gravy, homegrown green beans, stuffing, and a wedge of pumpkin pie.

Aunt Peg had broken off an aloe leaf, rubbed the gel on Ryan's sore palm, and bandaged the hand with a piece of white gauze. *Just like Anne would have done,* Kara thought. She was surprised at how much she missed Anne. The Nez Perce woman had become more than just a housekeeper and cook. She was a close friend as well—almost like a second mom.

Kara's thoughts were interrupted when Aunt Peg offered her a second piece of pie. Kara groaned and clutched her stomach. "Thanks, but I can't squeeze in one more bite."

Aunt Peg grinned. "I'll save you a piece of pumpkin pie for later tonight."

Ryan followed Dad and Grandpa into the living room, and Kara heard him begging to watch a movie. "Not now, Tiger," Dad said. Then they heard the voice of an announcer yelling, "A swing and a miss, and the Giants close out the second inning with the score San Francisco three, the Mariners nothing."

Kara peeked into the living room. "Isn't it a little early for baseball?" she asked Aunt Peg.

Aunt Peg chuckled. "Not down here. This is where a lot of the teams hold spring training. It must be an exhibition game."

Kara carried a stack of dishes to the sink. "Oh. I guess I'm just surprised Dad's watching it. He hasn't watched baseball, or any sports on TV, since Mom died."

Aunt Peg cleared her throat. "Well, then I think it's about time he did, don't you?" She loaded the last dirty plate into the dishwasher and turned it on, then poured another cup of coffee.

"Come sit." She patted the chair closest to her at the kitchen table. "Tell me about Wakara. Are you doing okay?"

Kara didn't have to ask what she meant. Aunt Peg wanted to know if she was getting over the grief of losing Mom.

"I'm okay. Most of the time," she admitted. "I mean, it's still really hard, but I don't cry as much as I used to." She focused on the brightly colored place mat under her coffee cup and felt tears form as Aunt Peg's hand covered her own.

Oh, right. I don't cry anymore. And I'm an excellent liar.

16

"You're healing. But it will still take time." Aunt Peg patted Kara's arm and took a sip of coffee.

"Anyway, from what your Dad tells me, you haven't exactly been sitting around brooding. A forest fire and a blizzard, all in three months' time."

Kara looked up and couldn't help but grin at her aunt's puzzled expression. "I guess it is pretty weird, isn't it? God's teaching me stuff though." She sighed. "It's just that sometimes I wish He'd slow it down a little."

Aunt Peg laughed. "Well, at your age, I would think you'd have all the time in the world to learn. He must be training you for something special."

"Whooeee, it's out of there! Didn't I tell you, Harley?" Grandpa Sheridan's voice boomed through the house and seemed to echo clear across the desert. "That rookie's an up-and-comer. I'll tell you now, he's going to take the Giants all the way to the pennant."

Dad's answering laugh held a spark of excitement Kara hadn't heard in awhile. "It sounds like they're really enjoying the game," she said.

Aunt Peg nodded. "Sure. If it's not baseball, it's football or basketball. Your grandfather's been watching sports every weekend since he's been here. He's done that since I was a child, and I don't suppose they broadcast much baseball in Ireland." Her expression softened. "It's good to have him home for a bit."

Kara decided to ask some of the questions that had been bothering her ever since she found out Grandpa was coming to the States. "Why'd he move to Ireland in the first place? We don't have relatives there anymore, do we?"

"That is exactly what he went to find out." Aunt Peg grabbed her sewing basket, picked up an embroidery hoop, and began working on a counted cross-stitch project. "I guess after Mama died he felt like he needed to find his roots, so to speak." She studied the pattern she had laid out on the table, then picked up her needle and began a new design.

Kara cleared her throat. "Well, did he? I mean, he's lived there so long."

Her aunt shrugged. "I'm not sure." She threaded the needle with several strands of Christmas Green. "I think he just fell in love with the place. Like I fell in love with Phoenix. I wouldn't go back to Portland if you paid me."

Kara winced. *And I wouldn't move to Phoenix if you gave me a million dollars.* But she kept that thought to herself. Instead, she decided to ask the question she'd been afraid to ask.

"Aunt Peg? Why did Grandpa come back now? He's not sick or anything, is he?"

"Sick?" Her aunt looked startled. "No. At least I don't think so." But she frowned as she folded the needlework and put it back in the basket. She thought a minute, then shook her head. "No. He made the decision to come right after I wrote him about your great-grandfather's trunk. It's been stored in my garage for years, but since I moved here, I really don't have room. I asked if he wanted me to send it to him or put it in storage. He called me the day after he got the letter and told me not to be in such a hurry, that he'd come and see to it himself."

She frowned again. "I did think that was a bit odd. But then, your grandfather always has had some strange ways." She laughed. "They say he inherited his stubborn, inquisitive streak from old Irish. Once he gets hold of an idea, he won't let it go."

She leaned closer, and Kara had to bend her head to hear. "He's been out in that garage every day since he arrived. I've hardly seen anything of him except his backside bending over that trunk. But when I go out there, he stuffs it all away and shuts the lid. Like I haven't had over thirty years to see it myself."

Kara grinned. "What's in it, Aunt Peg? What's the deep, dark secret?"

Aunt Peg actually snorted, and Kara swallowed hard to stifle a laugh. "You'll have to ask him that—if he'll tell you. I can't get a straight answer out of him. All I've seen are books and papers and stuff." She looked a bit sheepish. "I guess I just never took the time to look very closely."

It was late Saturday night before Kara had a chance to ask Grandpa Sheridan about the trunk. He narrowed his eyes, looked at the ceiling, and then busied himself lighting his pipe.

"All in good time, Wakara. All in good time."

3

"THAT'S ALL HE WOULD SAY!" Kara told Tia later on the phone. "'All in good time.' I wish I knew what that means."

"It means he's hiding something." Tia's voice dropped to a whisper. "Like, do you think it's got something to do with your Great-grandma Wakara?"

Kara felt a tingle of excitement. "Exactly. I'd give up riding for a week to find out what those papers say."

"Oh, sure." Tia's tone was sarcastic, and Kara had to smile. "You've been home exactly two hours, and I'll bet you've already ridden Lily all over the pasture."

Kara grinned even though Tia couldn't see her. "No, the meadow, and partway up the trail. I had to get back to help Colin clean the barn."

Tia laughed.

"Anyway," Kara continued, "Grandpa told me he still remembers my Great-grandmother Wakara. That made me feel good. Grandpa Sheridan is seventy-five. It made me realize that no matter how old I get, I'll still remember Mom."

"Well, sure." There was silence on the line, and then Tia cleared her throat. "Does your Gramps like Phoenix? Does he still have an Irish accent?"

Kara sighed. She and Tia talked about everything. When Kara's mom had died in a fiery car crash, Tia had been there for her with hugs and flowers, or she would just sit and hold Kara's hand. Tia would always listen, but talking about death was hard for her. "I just don't know what to say," she'd confessed one day. "I'm sorry, Wakara. I hope I'm still your best friend."

"You'll always be my best friend," Kara had reassured her. And that was still true today.

"Wakara? Are you still there?"

"Oh. Sorry, Tia. Sure, he likes Phoenix. Especially the early spring baseball games. And yes, he still has an accent when he wants to." She laughed. "Dad calls it pouring on the blarney."

Kara dragged the phone cord across the room and plopped cross-legged onto her bed, where she could see out the window. Dad was in the driveway, tinkering with the engine of his pickup truck. "You should have seen them together, Tia. Dad was loving it. I haven't seen him that happy in a long time. I wish Grandpa could have come home with us, but he promised to visit us again before he goes back to Ireland."

Tia sighed. "Wow, it must have been a cool trip. When are you watching that movie?"

Kara laughed again. "Tonight. And yes, you're invited. I think Anne cooked roast beef for dinner. I'll tell her to add another potato."

"Carrots?"

Kara rolled her eyes. "Always."

"Cool! See you in a few."

The line went dead. Kara hung up the phone and gazed back out the window. Ryan was racing his remote control car up and down the gravel driveway. The wind had picked up a little and blew the fringes of shaggy, blond hair off his

21

forehead. *He needs a haircut,* she thought automatically, *and I should make him put on a sweater.* But she knew he would argue, and in all fairness, she hadn't even needed a jacket this morning when she'd exercised Lily.

She opened the window and inhaled the fresh, clean air. She loved living in the Northwest, rain, snow, and all. Phoenix was okay for Aunt Peg, but no way did Kara ever want to live there.

A flash of sunlight bounced off the shiny plastic on Ryan's car as it raced by. Kara smiled, then listened as she heard the crunch of hooves on gravel. She leaned out and looked down the drive just as Greg and Colin came around the corner leading two horses. Her stomach did a little twist at the sound of Colin's laughter. His blond hair was hidden underneath a beat-up Stetson. The hat was pulled down enough so she couldn't see his wide, brown eyes, but she knew how the green specks sparkled when he smiled.

Greg was laughing too, and Kara felt a flutter of relief. It must have been a good ride. His riding helmet dangled from his right hand, and he led the horse, a spirited Arabian named Lyman, easily with his left. Her brother's speech had returned to normal, and even though he still had headaches and spells of feeling weak, he was pretty much the same as before the accident.

"You're lucky," the doctor had said. "When they first brought you in, I would have bet you'd never talk again."

Greg just grinned. "Not luck, Doc. I had a lot of people praying for me."

Kara felt a surge of pride, just thinking about it. The doctor had been impressed enough to answer, "Well, somebody up there is looking out for you."

And Greg had answered, "Not somebody, Doc. God."

Greg's horse, Lyman, danced a little as they passed Ryan, who was fiddling with the remote for his toy car. Kara almost called out a warning, but Ryan stood still, and the horse settled down.

A couple of months ago, Greg had decided he wanted to ride again. He'd picked out this horse at an auction. Kara winced. It wouldn't have been her choice. The young Arabian would tolerate a saddle and rider, but he wasn't very well trained. He was nervous and spooked easily—not a good choice for someone like Greg who was used to riding the sturdy, bombproof ranch horses. But Dad had agreed with Greg, thinking that Greg needed a challenge—something to boost his spirits—and training a new horse could be just the thing.

As they led the horses past the house, Colin looked up at her window and waved. Kara's smile froze as she heard the whir of rubber tires spitting gravel. She gasped as Ryan's black roadster went hurtling down the drive, hit a rock, and spun out right under the horses' feet.

It happened so fast, it took her breath away. Dakota side-hopped, knocking Colin into the bushes. Lyman went ballistic. She watched in horror as Greg tried to hang on to the reins with his weak arm, but the horse reared. His front hooves flailed just inches from Greg's face, then he broke away and bolted for the barn.

Kara didn't wait to see the outcome. She raced down the stairs and out the front door.

Dad got there ahead of her. He went straight to Greg and began examining his arm. Kara laid one hand on Ryan's shoulder and took away the remote control. The car lay smashed in the middle of the driveway. Ryan's eyes were wide with shock. Kara breathed a prayer of thanks that Dad was here. She was too worried about Colin and Greg to deal with her little brother.

Colin had jumped up, and he had Dakota under control. The big buckskin trembled when Kara went over and

23

rubbed a hand against his neck, but he held steady under Colin's examination.

"I think he's fine." Colin moved around his horse, looking for any obvious injuries.

Kara was winded from running and sucked in air. "What about you?" she asked.

"Nothing broken."

His eyes were still roaming over Dakota, and Kara didn't know if he meant himself or the horse.

They heard a sharp whinny, then a thud.

"Lyman!" Kara could hear the panic in Greg's voice, and then Dad's firm command, "Stay still, Son, I'm not through . . ."

She spun around and sprinted toward the barn, where she found Lyman, sides heaving, blowing foam and kicking at the metal sliding door. She stopped, then moved slowly toward his shoulder, talking softly. "Hey, boy, it's okay. You're safe now. Nothing's going to hurt you." *Gently,* she reminded herself, *like singing a baby to sleep.*

When Lyman caught sight of her, he threw his head, rolled his eyes, and stamped the ground. Then he banged the metal door again with one front foot.

"All right, boy," Kara crooned and inched closer. "I'll let you in. Just be still."

He moaned under his breath and jerked when she caught his headstall, but a few seconds of silent pressure and he lowered his head. His ears came forward, and Kara could feel his muscles relax under her hand.

She clucked softly and backed him up, then carefully slid open the door and led him into the barn. Once she got him on the grooming mat, she slipped off the headstall and replaced it with a halter. She took the saddle off, grabbed an armful of hay, and let him eat while she examined him.

24

He startled once when Colin came in leading Dakota. "You'd better put him in crossties, Wakara."

Colin's voice was calm, but she could hear the censure in his tone and felt a flash of irritation. She'd been working with horses a lot longer than Colin had, so what made him the expert?

"Crossties will only make him nervous." She moved slowly, running her hands along the horse's flank and down his legs. He winced and jerked away when she rubbed the tendon just above his right rear hoof. She looked closer and found a slight cut on the inside of his fetlock.

"It's not bad," she said when Colin squatted down next to her. "Just a surface wound. Will you please hold him a minute?"

Colin's eyes sparkled with humor. "Yes, Ma'am," he drawled, "I'd be happy to oblige." He grinned, then pushed to his feet and took hold of Lyman's halter.

Kara lifted the hoof and flexed it. The Arabian snorted, but didn't pull away. "I don't think there's any tendon damage. Let's walk him around a little."

"And take him away from his dinner?"

Colin's tone sounded sarcastic, but when she stood up, he flashed her a look of wide-eyed innocence. "What?"

She put her hands on her hips and glared at him. "Colin Jones, if you don't want to help . . ."

"What's going on? Is he okay?" Greg's worried voice interrupted her.

Colin steadied Lyman, and Kara turned to her brother. His face was white, but he moved past her, rubbing his hands over the horse's back and side.

"He's fine. Just a slight cut."

Greg looked at Colin, who nodded in agreement. "Wakara checked him out. We were just going to walk him around."

Greg looked relieved. "Okay." He nodded in her direction. "Thanks, Sis. I owe you one."

You don't owe me anything. Kara felt a twist of sadness. Greg was four years older than she was and they had never been close, but he was her brother and she loved him. He didn't have to pay her back. But she kept her thoughts to herself.

Greg's left arm trembled a little as he clipped a lead rope to the horse's halter.

"What about you?" She fixed her eyes on his face. "Are you okay?"

He nodded. "I'm fine. Just shook me up a little."

She and Colin stepped out of the way as he turned the horse around and led him to the door. "I'll walk him. You watch." He led Lyman out of the barn and down the driveway. Kara looked at Colin. He shrugged, grabbed his hat from the top of a hay bale, and trotted after them.

As Greg walked Lyman, they could see that the horse had only a slight limp. Greg turned down Kara's offer to dress the cut and did it himself. While Colin took off Dakota's saddle and measured grain into the feed pans, she added some wood shavings to Lyman's stall and filled the feeder with another pad of hay.

Two stalls down, Lily nickered for attention. Kara rubbed her down and fed her, then did the same for Ryan's pony, Star, adding a scoop of glucosamine to his grain. The pony was over eighteen years old and had developed some arthritis, but Ryan still rode him once in a while. Last year they had taken him to Eagle Lodge for the season so the younger kids could ride him. Dad had said they might leave him home this year, though, and Ryan had had a fit.

Kara sighed. Ry was really in for it this time. He'd been raised on this ranch and knew the rules. She couldn't believe he'd been careless enough to run that car while the horses were in the driveway. She looked around. The barn chores were done. Greg and Colin had put all the tack away and just stood there watching her.

Colin cleared his throat. "Uh, well, I've got some stuff to do in the bunkhouse. Guess I'll see you guys later. I may not make it in to dinner." He tipped his hat and started for the door.

"Wait up." Greg started after him. "I'd better get some homework done. I've got an early class on Monday." He glanced at her, then looked away. "Tell Dad I think I'll hit the hay early tonight. My arm's a little sore."

Kara couldn't believe it. "Wait a minute! What's with you guys? Anne's making a special dinner, and we're supposed to watch that tape, remember?" Then it hit her. *Those cowards!* They knew Ryan was in trouble, and they didn't want to be around for any punishment. Dad would surely make him apologize to both of them, and Kara knew from experience how uncomfortable that could be. She ran to catch up with them, but before she could get the barn door closed, a horn honked in the driveway.

Kara spun around, startled when she saw the slender, dark-haired girl in a short, ribbed T-shirt and blue jeans walking toward her carrying a small, brown shopping bag. "Hey, Wakara, wait, I brought some carrots for Lily and Star."

Tia! With all the commotion, she had forgotten her friend was coming for dinner, and she hadn't even told Anne, let alone Dad.

4

WHILE TIA FED CARROT PIECES to the four horses in the barn, Kara explained what had happened with Ryan's remote control car.

"Wow!" Tia exclaimed. "That could have spelled disaster. Is your dad really mad?"

"I don't know," Kara sighed. "I haven't been up to the house yet. And Colin and Greg are trying to get out of dinner altogether—the cowards."

Tia rolled her eyes. "Well, if everyone's in a mood, I guess I could call Pops and have him come get me."

That's probably a good idea. But Tia looked so disappointed, Kara didn't have the heart to tell her what she was thinking. Instead she said, "Let's go see. Maybe everything's quieted down by now."

"Yea. Like, maybe your little brother is grounded 'til he's twenty-one."

Kara had to laugh. Tia was right. Ry was always getting into trouble. Mom had called him "an accident waiting to happen." But Kara sure hoped he'd outgrow it before he turned twenty-one.

They went around to the back door and found Anne in the kitchen, taking the roast out of the oven.

"Tia." Anne smiled as she spooned carrots, potatoes, and onions out of the pan into serving bowls. "There is plenty."

Tia and Kara grinned at each other. Leave it to Anne; she was always prepared. Kara noticed the table was already set. "Sorry I wasn't around to help," she said.

"You were needed elsewhere." Anne adjusted her colorful shirt, pulling it down over her too-snug jeans. "For six months I move like the grasshopper. Now I must work like the ant."

Kara and Tia both laughed. Anne had gained some weight while her broken leg was healing. She was trying to work it off, but Kara knew the older woman still had bouts of pain in her leg when she was on her feet too much.

"We'll clean up," Kara offered. Tia nodded in agreement.

Dad and Ryan came through the kitchen door. Ryan took his place at the table and wouldn't look at anyone. Dad greeted the girls, but Kara noticed the sparkle that had been in his eyes for the past few days was gone.

"Uh," she said, "Colin and Greg said to tell you they might not make it to dinner."

Dad frowned. "Where are they?"

"At the bunkhouse." Kara grabbed Tia's arm and dragged her toward the kitchen doorway. "We'd better go wash up."

When they came back down ten minutes later, Anne was alone in the kitchen, and all the serving platters were covered with aluminum foil.

Tia groaned. "Where'd everybody go? I'm starved!" She reached for a homemade roll, and Kara nearly lost it when the quiet, unflappable, Nez Perce woman actually tapped Tia's hand with the back of a serving spoon.

"We wait," Anne said calmly.

Tia's mouth dropped open. Then she looked at Kara, and they both burst out laughing.

"What's so funny?" Ryan bounced into the room, followed by Dad, Colin, and Greg.

Kara threw Tia a look of relief. *They must have settled it.* After the blessing, Dad started a conversation about their trip to Phoenix, and Kara knew she was right.

Kara let the conversation flow around her. It was too bad Grandpa and Aunt Peg couldn't be here, but it was so nice to have the rest of the family together at the table. She buttered a roll and felt a sense of contentment that she hadn't felt in a long time.

The talk died down, and everyone was busy eating. While eating her own meal, Anne passed the serving dishes as soon as someone was out of food. Only Ryan kept up a constant chatter between bites of roast beef smothered in catsup.

Colin had taken off his hat, and Kara had to smile at the lock of damp, brown hair plastered to his forehead. *He must have just washed it.* She wanted to reach over and brush it away from his eyes. There was a nick on his chin from his razor, and he'd missed a few tiny hairs right along his jaw. Instead of shoveling in food like he usually did, he kept one hand on his lap and ate slowly, one bite at a time. He was quieter than usual, too, and Kara wondered if he felt uncomfortable after the episode with Ryan. Maybe she should say something; start another conversation.

Before she could think of something to say, Colin looked up and flashed her a grin that caused deep dimples in his cheeks. *Tia's right. He really does have a killer smile.*

"Wakara, is something wrong? You've barely touched your food." Dad's voice seemed to echo through the now silent kitchen.

Kara jumped. "What? No. I mean, it's great. I guess I'm just not very hungry." Everyone was staring at her. Her fork clattered against her plate, then fell to the floor. The heat spread from her stomach to her neck and face, and she wanted to crawl under the table.

"I'll get it." Ryan jumped out of his chair, whacking her shin with his cowboy boot.

Instant tears stung her eyes. *This is not happening*, she thought as her little brother scooted underneath her chair, nearly knocking her over, then scrambled out again and handed her the fork.

"Don't cry, Kara. Just wipe it off with your napkin, and it'll be good as new."

That was exactly what Mom would have said to him. Everyone laughed and went back to eating, but Kara still felt like she was living a nightmare. Worse, Dad was still watching her with that thoughtful, *What's-going-on-with-her?* expression on his face. More than anything she wanted to ask to be excused, but that would only draw more attention, which was exactly what she wanted to avoid!

A gentle hand squeezed her shoulder as Anne handed her a clean fork. She managed to eat a few more bites of dinner, but the beef tasted stringy, and her carrots were cold.

Ryan swallowed the last of his milk and jumped to his feet. "Hey, everybody, hurry up. We get to see the movie now!" He ran from the room, and Kara could hear him rummaging through the tape drawer below the VCR. She started to call out and tell him to wait, but Dad held up his hand.

"I'll get him in a minute." His voice was quiet, but firm. "Anne, Ryan is to clear the table and load the dishwasher for a week." He shook his head. "I'm sorry, I know it means more work than if you did it yourself, but I'd appreciate it if you'd supervise him."

He cleared his throat and looked at Kara. "Wakara, please see to it that he makes his bed and puts his clothes in the hamper every morning before he goes to school. And I mean *he's* to do it. Don't give in and do it yourself, even if it takes more time. Deal?"

"Deal." She sighed. "But what if it makes us late for school?"

"If he doesn't get it done, you both leave for the bus on time, and I'll take care of it when he gets home."

Kara glanced at Tia, but she was examining the ceiling as if she'd never seen one before, and Colin kept his head down, concentrating on his empty plate.

Dad's gaze switched to Greg, and her older brother let out a groan. Dad smiled and laid a hand on Greg's shoulder. "He has to learn some responsibility, Son. And since you're training that high-spirited colt of yours, I think you're the one to teach him more respect for horses."

Greg looked as shocked as Kara felt. Up 'til now, it had been her responsibility to teach Ryan to ride and groom the horses. She had started his lessons last fall, but then he took Star out without permission and lost his riding privileges.

Dad must have read her mind. "I don't mean I want him riding Lyman. Wakara can handle the riding lessons with Star. But it won't hurt him to learn how to lead and back up a horse. Just once a week or so, until he gets the hang of it. Use the round pen—it's safer."

"Hey, you guys, come on." Ryan raced in and grabbed Colin's arm. "You gotta see this movie; it's awesome."

Kara could tell Colin was trying not to laugh. He ran one hand through his hair, brushing the stray lock off his forehead, then used his best Texas drawl. "Well, Partner, I think you've got some chores to finish first."

Ryan followed Colin's arm as it swept over the table full of dirty dishes. His face crumpled, and Kara was sure he was going to cry. Instead, he sighed and handed the tape to Dad. "Oh. I forgot." He turned to Anne. "I'll do dishes tonight, Anne. You'd better sit and put your foot up so it don't get sore."

5

DAD WAS RIGHT, OF COURSE. The film was not nearly as exciting without the special screen and 3-D projector. But Kara still felt the thrill of flying high over the Grand Canyon, plunging deep into the churning river, then floating through the misty shadows into brilliant light.

"Outrageous!" Tia shouted when the film was over.

Everyone stared at her, and Kara laughed. "Outrageous?"

Tia just grinned. "Sure. And if you don't know, Miss 4.0 student, it means amazing, marvelous, impressive, and sensational!"

"It also means shocking, monstrous, and excessive," Kara grinned back. "I had the same vocabulary track in English last year."

Tia rolled her eyes. "Whatever." She looked at Kara's dad. "Have you ever flown over something that awesome, Mr. S.?"

Dad shook his head. "No. I would have liked to, but no one's allowed to fly over or into the Grand Canyon anymore except for rescue helicopters."

Tia still had that dreamy look that came over her when she latched onto an idea. "Can you imagine exploring a place like that? I mean, like, I wouldn't want to mess with the scorpions and snakes and stuff, but it would be so awesome to go in there just for a couple of days and see how those people lived, you know?"

"I'd take my raft in." Colin's voice rang with almost as much excitement as Tia's. "Man, what a rush!"

Kara shook her head. "That would be a rush, all right. I don't see how any of those explorers survived. Those rapids were worse than class five. I'll bet they weren't even on the chart!"

Colin laughed. "Rapids probably weren't even rated back then. Now it's one through five—ripples through raging white water." He shook his head. "Threes and fours are good enough for me. Only a crazy man would tackle a class five."

"You could hike in," Ryan piped up. "There's a trail for angels, but they let mules and people use it too, I saw!"

Kara reached over and ruffled his hair. "You mean Angel Trail?"

"Yeah."

"Angel is the name of the trail, Ry. And they take mules down almost every day." She sighed. "It looked like fun, but we didn't have time."

"Too crowded," Tia insisted. "At least it was when Pops took us a few years ago. We went to Mesa Verde too, and I saw how the Anasazi Indians lived. They built homes right into the sides of the cliffs and farmed the flat spots up above."

"The Anasazi disappeared." Everyone turned to look at Anne, who was sitting in the far corner of the room next to her loom. "Hundreds of years they live in the canyons, then they are gone." Her face was calm, but Kara could hear a trace of sadness in her voice.

Tia nodded. "Yeah. They just vanished overnight." She looked at Kara. "Wouldn't it be awesome to find out why?"

"Some things only God can know," Anne said as she rose and headed for the kitchen. "I will bring the pie."

"I'll help." Kara uncurled herself from the couch where she'd been sitting beside Ryan and Greg.

"Me too." Tia jumped up from her spot on the floor. "What kind of pie?"

While Tia got down the plates, Kara rummaged through the dishwasher for clean forks, and Anne cut into the deep-dish apple pie. She handed two plates to Kara, then held out two more for Tia to take into the family room, but she didn't let go of them right away. "Wakara's grandfather called while you were at the barn, Tia. He would like to read your paper on the Northern California Indian tribes."

Kara couldn't wait to talk to Tia alone, but by the time they finished dessert, Tia's dad had arrived to pick her up.

"Your grandfather is looking for something, just like we are!" Tia whispered when Kara walked her to the front porch.

Kara nodded. "I think he already knows more than he's telling." She frowned. "It's frustrating. He's had months to go through Great-grandfather's papers. If he knows something new about my great-grandmother, I wish he'd tell me."

"Maybe he just wants to be sure first. You know, like, have all the facts before he tells you."

Kara shrugged, then gave Tia a quick hug. "Thanks, friend."

"Hey, no prob. See you tomorrow." Tia grinned and hurried to the car.

Kara drew in a deep breath of the cool night air and tipped her head back to study the stars. *The night sky—another one of God's masterpieces.* "Outrageous," she whispered to herself, then she chuckled. Tia could be weird sometimes, but no one could ask for a better friend.

"Wakara?" Colin's voice interrupted her thoughts. Light filtered through the open door, then vanished as Colin closed it behind him. She shivered a little when he walked up and stood beside her. "Aren't you cold?"

She shook her head. If she tried to talk, she was afraid her voice would shake too. *Knock it off, Wako, it's just Colin.* Right, if it was "just Colin," why did she feel all jittery inside?

Colin walked past her, turned around, and leaned backwards against the railing, his head thrown back until he was practically upside down.

Kara giggled and finally found her voice. "What are you doing?"

"The Milky Way, see?" He pointed to the sky over the steeply pitched roof, then motioned her to stand beside him.

She laughed. "Why don't you just go out into the yard? You could see it better from there."

"This is a lot more fun. Come on, try it." He reached for her hand and pulled her to the railing.

Kara took her place beside him and leaned back, craning her neck to spot the Milky Way. But the fluttering in her stomach had nothing to do with a band of stars.

"Colin? Wakara?" The front door opened again, and this time the porch light flicked on. Kara blinked and jumped away from the railing as if it was on fire. "Hey, sorry," Greg said. She could hear the chuckle in her brother's voice as he reached out to steady her. "Dad wants you guys in the house. Family meeting."

Greg held the door for her, and she rushed into the family room. Dad watched her with that thoughtful look again, and motioned for her to sit down. Ryan sat on the floor in front of the TV, sorting through his box of John Wayne movie tapes.

When Colin and Greg came in, Dad said, "Thanks, guys, this won't take long." He looked around the room, his face sober.

Kara felt a stab of fear. *Was something wrong?*

Dad cleared his throat. "I know we just returned from a long weekend, but spring break is just around the corner."

He paused and grinned. "How would you all like to spend the week at Eagle Lodge?"

"Yippee!" Ryan jumped up and spun around the room, nearly knocking over Colin, who squatted on his heels by the door.

Greg stood beside Colin, leaning against the wall. "Yeah, yippee for you," he said with a trace of sarcasm in his voice. "I have a feeling that for the rest of us it means work." Kara hadn't heard him use that tone in a long time, but at least now he was smiling.

Dad laughed. "I'm afraid Greg is right. It won't be just a pleasure trip. We've got a lot of extra work to do because of the fire."

Stuff they didn't get done last fall because of the storm that practically shut down the ranch—the same blizzard that nearly killed Greg. Kara kept her thoughts to herself. She didn't want to bring up bad memories.

It had gotten quiet in the room, and Kara realized Dad was staring at her. She blushed. She'd been daydreaming again. "Sorry, Dad. What did you say?"

"I just wondered if this upsets any plans you had for spring break."

She thought a minute, then stole a glance at Colin. A bunch of kids from youth group were planning a rafting trip, and Colin had said he would come and bring his new four-man raft. "We did have plans," she said aloud, "but I guess we could do it another time." She tried to keep the disappointment out of her voice. Eagle Lodge was a main source of income for their family, and Dad needed all the help he could get to keep it running. Besides, she really liked it there. Sure, it was a lot of work, but the lodge itself was comfortable, and the wilderness that surrounded it was nothing short of spectacular. At least it used to be, before the forest fire. When she'd been up there last, there was so

37

much snow she hadn't been able to tell how much of the forest had been destroyed by the flames.

Tia would be really disappointed, though. They'd planned on going shopping for some summer clothes.

"Tia would be a help, I think," Anne said. Kara looked at Anne, astonished, then felt a rush of gratitude when Dad nodded.

"Yes." His eyes shifted to Colin, then quickly back to Kara. "I think that would be a good idea. If her parents agree, she can come along and help."

Dad slapped his knees and stood. "Okay, then, we leave a week from Friday." He glanced at Anne. "Is that enough notice?"

The cook nodded. "We will all go?"

"Yes," Dad answered. "You can close up the house. Bud Davis will send some hands to take care of the stock." He turned to Colin and Greg. "We'll need horses. You can bring your own and lead a couple of others."

Ryan leapt to his feet. "Star gets to come!"

Dad wrapped one arm around Ryan's skinny shoulders. "Not this time, Tiger."

Ryan's face clouded up and Kara expected him to argue, but he must have realized it wouldn't do any good. He just hung his head and went back to sorting his tapes.

Colin stood up, and Greg clapped a hand on his shoulder. "Is that it?" He looked at Dad, who nodded. "Good. I don't know about you," he said to Colin, "but I'm headed for the bunkhouse. I've got a class tomorrow morning, and 5:00 A.M. comes early."

Kara glanced at the clock and groaned out loud. Ryan should have been in bed an hour ago. Now he'd be a bear when she tried to get him up for school tomorrow. She kissed Dad goodnight. "Come on, Ry, I'll race you up the stairs."

She let him win, of course, and smiled when he ran into the bathroom and locked the door behind him. She remembered when she was about the same age and wanted privacy. Mom hadn't said anything, just backed off and allowed her to become more independent every year.

"He's growing up, Mom," she whispered. "I know I can't do as good a job as you would, but I'll try."

Ryan changed into his cowboy pajamas and fell asleep before Kara could remind him to say his prayers.

Kara brushed her teeth, undid her braids, and pulled her long, black hair over one shoulder so she could untangle it with the brush. Just thinking about all she had to do in the next few days made her tired. First thing tomorrow morning, she would invite Tia to come with them to Eagle Lodge.

She was really disappointed to miss the rafting trip, especially since she'd planned on manning the oar opposite Colin in his raft. Maybe there'd still be time for a river run before the spring season was over. She yawned at the mirror, set the brush aside, and headed for her room.

Her closet door stood open, reminding her of the shopping trip she would have to postpone. Most of her summer clothes had smoke damage from the forest fire. She'd managed to save a couple pair of shorts, but everything else was terminal, and that included most of Ryan's things as well. She groaned and promised herself she'd have a talk with Dad in the morning. Maybe he could take them to the mall the Saturday after they got back.

Her head was spinning when she laid it on the pillow. *Be anxious for nothing.* The Bible verse popped into her mind. *But in everything by prayer and supplication with thanksgiving let your requests be made known unto God.*

Prayer always worked when she asked God to help with the big things, like rescuing people from fire and snow. Was it true He cared about the little things as well? She knew Mom and Anne thought so.

She whispered a prayer, mentally giving everything she was worried about to God and thanking Him ahead of time for the answer. Then she turned on her side and closed her eyes.

6

KARA MET TIA ON THE school steps as usual, ten minutes before the first class.

"You'll never guess!" Tia squealed. "Never in a zillion years!"

Kara couldn't guess, but it didn't matter, because Tia didn't give her a chance to answer. "We did it, Wakara. Patches and I made the cut."

This time Kara squealed. "You're in with Mrs. Bryant?"

Tia's grin would have outshone the moon. "Only the best barrel racer in the country." She grabbed Kara's arm. "And, the best part is, we're one-on-one!"

"Private lessons?" Kara was shocked. Mrs. Bryant only took on private students when she thought they had exceptional talent. Was Tia really that good?

Tia was bobbing her head as if Kara had spoken out loud. "She said Patches and I have done a good job on the preliminaries. She said he's fast and well trained—no, she said he's *very* well trained, thank you very much, and we have this bond—sort of like ESP, you know? And that's, like, really important. She thinks we have what it takes." Tia shouted over the blare of the first bell. "Rodeo circuit here I come!"

Kara laughed as Tia danced her in a circle, then linked arms

41

and pulled her through the open doorway into the crowded hall.

Kara was excited for her, but if Tia was starting barrel racing lessons with Mrs. Bryant, she might not be able to go with them to Eagle Lodge. *Well, there's no time to talk about it now,* Kara thought as the bell rang a second time.

"Yipes," Tia squealed. "I can't be late again. See you at lunch!"

Kara took out her history book, stored her backpack in her locker, and walked ten feet down the hall to the most boring class of the day.

At noon, she carried her lunch tray to the table where Tia was burning her boyfriend Devon's ears about Patches, barrel racing, and rodeos. Devon rolled his eyes at Wakara in greeting. She grinned and shrugged her shoulders. What could she do? When Tia got this excited about something, you just had to let her get it out of her system. The news about Eagle Lodge would have to wait.

After school, Kara waited for Ryan. She always let him choose his own seat on the bus and usually he sat with some of his friends, but today he took the seat next to her. By the time they reached their stop along the rural road, Kara's ears rang from his constant chatter.

Greg had promised their little brother he could help with Lyman for half an hour, and Ryan was so excited he jumped the last step off the bus and raced on ahead. Kara held her breath until he was safely over the slick, wooden bridge, then sighed and followed him across.

It had rained off and on during the day, adding a shimmer of silver to the tumbling river and shining up the new spring leaves. She usually felt a thrill at the first signs of tulips and daffodils sprouting from the once-frozen ground; she loved spring with its cycle of rebirth. Mom always called March and April "the renaissance months."

A time of new beginnings when creation portrayed Christ's death and resurrection.

But today for some reason, Kara felt anything but renewed, as if new beginnings were for everyone but her. Tia was moving on from trail rides to barrel races. Ryan would learn to work with horses while Greg trained Lyman.

As she moved closer to the house, she sighed. Mom always said self-pity was a pit you'd be wise to walk around. Well, today it felt like she was balancing right on the edge of the pit. She felt tears sting her eyes and swiped them away with the back of her hand. What was wrong with her, anyway? She was fifteen years old, and the past eighteen months had brought her enough new challenges to last a lifetime.

Anne came out of the kitchen as Kara hung her jacket on the rack in the entry hall. She said nothing, and Kara almost ran by her up the stairs, but she stopped when she caught a glimpse of the woman's kind smile. Kara sighed and forced herself to turn around. "Do you need any help with dinner?"

"No. It is almost done." The concern on Anne's face made Kara want to cry again, but instead of asking Kara if she wanted to talk, which she didn't, Anne nodded toward the window. "You must hurry if you want to ride before dark."

Kara could have hugged her. Instead, she flashed her a watery smile and rushed up to her room to change.

Lily's apricot-colored coat smelled warm and sweet as Kara brushed her. Then Kara quickly threw on a bareback pad. She slipped a bit into her horse's mouth, gathered the reins, and led her to the mounting block.

Kara was already on her horse before she remembered she'd left her helmet hanging on a hook next to the tack room door. She started to dismount, then changed her mind. What could happen? They weren't going very far.

Whatever her problems, Kara always felt better once she was on Lily's back. She waved at Ryan and Greg, who were putting Lyman through his paces in a smaller round pen behind the barn, then clucked softly, urging her horse into a fast walk until they reached the open meadow. Then she balanced herself, gripping with her thighs as the mare cantered across the rain-slick grass.

Kara didn't know about ESP, but she'd been riding Lily for so long that the horse seemed to know what she wanted before she asked. The mare was fast and surefooted. They would do well together at barrel racing. Tia had been trying for months to coax her into doing something like that, but there was just no time.

Anne had taken up a lot of the slack at home, but Kara still had responsibilities with Ryan and around the ranch. Then their summers were spent at Eagle Lodge. Rodeo and riding clubs were out for her, but she didn't really mind. She much preferred working with stock on the ranch and helping Colin, Dad, and Greg when the need arose. Tia had always been around to help, but now her friend would not only have Devon to share her time with, but riding lessons and competition too.

Am I jealous? she asked herself as she turned Lily in a circle and brought her up beside the tree line at the north end of the meadow. "No," she said aloud. She stroked Lily's neck. "I think I'm just feeling a little left out."

Lily's answering whinny seemed to say, "I agree." Kara laughed. She knew the horse was only telling her to get on with the ride.

The distance from one end of the meadow to the other was at least two hundred yards—the length of two football fields. The mare was still young and spirited, and this was a great place to let her run.

"Okay, girl. Here we go." She leaned forward and squeezed Lily's sides with her legs. The horse broke into a lope, then a full gallop. Kara held the reins loose and low on the horse's neck, closed her eyes, and lost herself in the rhythm of the ride. If she threw her arms out it would be like flying—even more exciting than buzzing the Grand Canyon in a plane.

Why not? Lily's gait was smooth and the ground fairly even. She wouldn't be taking too much of a chance. The reins were already knotted so they wouldn't fall; all she had to do was let go.

She dropped the reins and sat up straight, barely slowing Lily's stride. When she had her balance, she spread her arms straight out and lifted her face to the wind. A rush of adrenaline left her light-headed. She closed her eyes and inhaled the sweet, damp air. It smelled of pine resin and rain-washed earth. "Ayiiee," she howled as tears of joy flooded her eyes. *I can do it. I can fly!* The heady rush of freedom was almost unbearable.

Too late, she felt the change in Lily's stride. The horse suddenly slowed, reared, then plunged sideways. Before she knew what was happening, Kara hit the ground.

The air rushed out of her lungs with a resounding whoosh. Her head reeled, and her ears buzzed like a nest of angry bees. She struggled for breath and managed to get onto her hands and knees. She could hear Lily's high-pitched whinny and the pounding of hooves as her horse ran away, but when she tried to lift her head, the world spun black. She instantly dropped it down again.

Something had caused Lily to spook. The horse sounded terrified. Kara's only conscious thought was to find out why. She drew in three slow, deep breaths, then carefully lifted her head. Her vision cleared, but one glance at the tree line in front of her and she froze. Fear shot like lightning bolts through her stomach and chest. For an instant she felt light-headed again. She fought down the nausea that welled up in her throat and tried to calm her pounding heart. *It's just a cub. A cute, fuzzy, little, black bear cub.* But cubs almost always have a mother close by, and that was not good news.

Think! She had to keep a clear head. She knew what to do. She and Colin had gone over it several times when they had taught a survival class at the high school last fall. If only her woozy brain would cooperate.

Slowly and carefully, she got to her feet and stood still until another wave of dizziness passed. Then she began to back away, keeping her eyes on the cub. It mewled and stared back at her with curious, dark brown eyes.

A deep-throated growl stopped Kara in her tracks. *Don't run!* "Oh, God, keep me calm. Please!" she cried out loud, then made herself turn toward the cub's angry mother. The sow wasn't very big, but Kara knew that size didn't matter to a mama bear defending her cub. Neither did size make the claws or teeth any less lethal.

The bear was about twenty feet away. It stood on two legs, sniffing the air and watching as Kara moved slowly backwards. If she could put Mama Bear between herself and the cub, it might make her seem like less of a threat.

But Mama Bear wasn't buying it. She suddenly dropped to all fours and huffed furiously, taking three quick strides toward Kara. Then she stopped as if waiting for her prey to react.

Kara stood her ground. She straightened up, making herself look as tall as possible, and waved her arms, yelling at the top of her lungs. "Go away! Go on, scram! Get out of here!"

The bear stayed where it was, rose up on two legs, and swung her head toward her cub. The little bear bleated and scampered toward her, but a deep-throated warning sent it scurrying up a tree.

While the bear was distracted, Kara looked around frantically. She had to have a weapon. Something to protect herself if the bear really charged.

A few feet away, a small, flat tree stump marked the place where last spring she and Greg and Dad had built a fire ring. Kara felt a surge of hope. She had gathered most of the rocks herself, and if she remembered right, they were big enough to pack quite a wallop.

The bear swung back toward her, shaking its head and clawing up clumps of earth. "Help me, God!" Kara cried as she lunged toward the tree stump, scooped up a rock, and threw it as hard as she could. It landed just short of the snarling animal. Yelling, screaming, and jumping up and down, she snatched up another rock, took aim, and threw. *Missed again!*

But the enraged bear took a step backwards, and Kara knew she couldn't let up. A picture flashed through her mind of her father and grandfather watching TV. *Baseball. Think baseball.* She'd been a good pitcher in the Kids' Sports league.

This time she forced herself to pause and take aim. She couldn't believe the bear still hadn't charged. She could feel the sweat beading up on her forehead, and her hands felt like they'd been greased with cooking oil. She went into her windup stance, then let loose with everything she had.

A screamer! The ball-sized rock split the air like a knife and plunged into the bear's belly with a resounding thwack. The animal froze, then went down. Kara's heart thudded like a drum as the bear rolled to her feet and ran away from Kara into the woods. *She won't be gone long,* Kara thought, *not with the cub still in that tree.*

A sharp whinny brought Kara around. Lily stood about thirty yards away, trembling and ready to bolt. In the far distance, Kara heard shouts and saw figures running toward her across the meadow. She lunged toward her horse, but Lily was still spooked and danced just out of reach. Not that it mattered. She couldn't mount bareback without help, and the only tree stump was too close to the bear. *Well, Wako, you wanted to fly. So fly!* She took a deep breath and sprinted toward the running men.

7

"It was my own fault, Dad. I wasn't paying attention." Kara accepted a cup of chamomile tea from Anne, but her hands were shaking so badly she nearly spilled it.

"Wakara, are you sure you're not injured?" The concern on Dad's face hurt more than the scrapes and bruises.

She nodded. "I'm okay, really. The fall knocked the wind out of me. Then I saw the bear . . ."

She shuddered. "I've never been so scared in my life."

"Mother bear is a formidable enemy," Anne said. "God was watching."

Kara agreed. "You've got that right. I can't believe she didn't charge! And that fire ring. We built it last year, remember, Dad? When I was helping you and Greg round up strays. The rocks were the perfect size and within reach. That wasn't an accident."

The door slammed as Colin and Greg came into the room, rifles still in their hands. "Sow's gone," Greg informed them. "So is the cub."

"No blood either," Colin added. "She must not have been hurt very badly."

Kara shook her head. "No, the rock hit her in the belly. I think it just knocked the wind out of her." She took a deep breath and blew it out on a long sigh. "Poor bear. I know how she feels."

Everyone laughed, and Kara could feel the tension in the room dissolve.

Ryan's feet were dangling from Dad's lap, but when the phone rang, he jumped up and dashed out of the room. Dad turned to Greg. "You boys store those guns, then get the stock fed. We can finish the branding tomorrow."

Colin nodded, but instead of leaving, he handed his rifle to Greg. "I'll be there in a minute." He moved to the sofa and squatted down in front of Kara until they were eye-to-eye. "I hope you don't plan on doing that again anytime soon." He gazed at her as if there were no one else in the room.

It's not like I planned it! Kara started to protest, then realized Colin wasn't blaming her, but telling her how scared he had been. She grinned and held up two fingers in a Girl Scout salute. "I promise to do my best to stay away from bears." The smile he gave her felt like a hug.

Dad cleared his throat. "She's fine, young man. I think you'd better get to those chores."

Colin stood, tipped his hat to Anne, and left the room.

"Dad!" Kara couldn't believe her ears. Dad could be firm sometimes, but he was never rude.

The phone was ringing again as Ryan bounded back into the room. Dad switched his attention to her little brother. "Aren't you going to answer that?"

Ryan shrugged. "Prob'ly not; it's just Tia, and I already tol' her she couldn't talk to Kara now because she's resting from almost getting eaten by a bear."

"Ryan Sheridan, you didn't!" Kara exclaimed.

Dad just stared at Ryan, then turned to Kara. She couldn't tell if he was going to laugh or cry. "Anne," he said, almost choking on the words, "would you please get the phone? I'm going upstairs."

"What's with him?"

Kara didn't realize she had said the words out loud until Ryan answered, "Maybe he's gotta go."

Anne flashed her a sympathetic look, then hurried from the room.

Kara hobbled to the phone and assured Tia everything was fine, then washed and went in to dinner. But by the time she had finished a small portion of vegetable soup and pushed away from the table, she realized she could hardly move without pain.

Anne helped her upstairs, ran hot water into the tub, and added an earthy smelling liquid.

"Juniper." She answered Kara's unspoken question. "You will soak twenty minutes now, then again before bed. The pain will be gone."

Kara groaned, crawled into the tub, and sank up to her neck into the hot mixture. The effect was so soothing she moaned again, this time with relief. "Oh, Anne, what would I do without you?"

Anne smiled, laid a fresh towel on the sink, and left the room.

When Kara woke up the next morning, she realized Anne had done it again. Her bruises were already fading to yellow, and most of the pain was gone. She managed to catch up with Tia before second period and was rewarded by her friend's excited squeal when she asked her about going with them to Eagle Lodge.

"We don't start with Mrs. Bryant until after Easter," Tia assured her. "I'll ask Pops, but I know they'll let me come.

My grades are so much better, they let me do practically anything I want."

By Thursday of the next week everything was arranged. Dad had decided that Kara could ride into the valley with Colin and Greg, but he hadn't sounded too happy about it. "I'd rather have you with me," he'd said without giving a reason why, "but we're going to need some extra mounts, and I don't want the guys to pony more than one apiece.

"Ryan has permission to leave school a day early," he continued without looking at her, "so he and Anne will come with me in the Cessna. Tia will fly in with Mark on Saturday when he brings the extra supplies."

Kara thought about that conversation as she followed Ryan from the bus stop down the narrow dirt road, then up the gravel drive. What was up with Dad? Every time he talked to her lately, his voice sounded sharp, and he wouldn't really look her in the eye.

"It's not like I've done anything wrong," she told Tia.

Tia shrugged. "I wouldn't worry about it. When Pops weirds out on us, it usually means he's had a bad day at work."

Kara nodded to be polite, but she didn't really think it had anything to do with the ranch. Maybe he was just missing Mom and didn't know how to handle it. Men weren't nearly as good at dealing with emotions as women were. She'd started paying attention when she'd learned that in Health class and found it was true. Maybe Tia was right. Maybe Dad's behavior didn't really have anything to do with her at all.

Ryan had stopped to smell a clump of wild snapdragons. "Don't pick them, Ry. The wild ones don't keep very well. Besides, we leave in the morning and won't be around to enjoy them." She urged him on ahead of her.

After dinner Ryan helped Anne clear the table, and Kara escaped to her room to fold laundry and pack. The weather was so unsettled this time of the year, she knew she would need to dress in layers. She'd have to go through Ryan's things too.

By the time she finished, Ryan was in bed and Dad had gone to his room. Colin had taken off for the bunkhouse without even looking at her.

The more she thought about it, the angrier she felt. Sure, she had messed up, riding recklessly and without a helmet. She'd apologized for that and promised not to do it again, but it wasn't her fault that the bear chose to park her cub at the edge of the meadow. That was no reason to treat her like—like fish bait!

A squeak of hinges and the rattle of silverware told her Anne was still in the kitchen emptying the dishwasher. Kara sighed. Mom always made sure the kitchen was spotless and the refrigerator cleaned out before they left on a trip, even if it was just a couple of days. Anne was like that too. In fact, Anne was like Mom in a lot of ways.

Kara zipped her duffel bag shut and hurried down the stairs. At the bottom, she hesitated when she heard voices in the kitchen. Maybe she shouldn't interrupt. Besides, she couldn't talk to Anne if someone else was around. She started to turn around and go back to her room, but Dad's voice caught her attention.

"Then you think I should tell her now? I wish I could be sure she will understand."

"Wakara is wise for one so young, but you must follow your heart."

Kara stood there stunned. Dad and Anne were talking about her! What did she need to understand? And why all the secrecy? Was this what had Dad and Colin acting so weird? She hesitated. Part of her wanted to run back to her room and forget what she had heard. But if something was wrong, she needed to know about it.

She turned toward the kitchen door just as Dad stepped out carrying a bundle of papers in one hand and a dingy brown, canvas-covered book in the other. When he saw her standing there, a flicker of dismay crossed his face. "Wakara." He shifted the papers to his other hand. "How much of that did you hear?"

Anne appeared in the doorway and shot her a reassuring smile. Kara decided to be honest. "Just the part about you not wanting to tell me something because you're afraid I won't understand, but Anne thinks I will."

Dad nodded. "I hope so." He motioned her into the kitchen. "We received a package from your grandfather today. He asked me to read the material, then give it to you." He nodded at Anne. "Would you please make a pot of decaf? This might take a while."

It might as well have been a double espresso, Kara thought an hour later as she took the bundle of papers and the canvas notebook up to her room. She would never sleep tonight anyway. She tossed her great-grandfather's journal on the bed, stared at her reflection in the mirror, and repeated her given name, "Wakara Windsong Sheridan." Her Yahi name.

She lifted the charcoal drawing of her great-grandmother from the wall, held it up next to her own face, and compared the features. Eyes and nose, the shape of her chin and brow, were identical. The first Wakara was certainly her ancestor. But Kara had always thought her great-grandmother was Nez Perce. Great-grandpa Irish had written a letter saying he had found the infant Wakara in the woods near a Nez Perce reservation. She had always believed that. But now, if what Dad and Grandpa had read in Irish Sheridan's journal was true, almost everything she thought she knew about her namesake was a lie.

8

THE BEAT OF A BOOT-STOMPING country song shocked Kara into awareness. She groaned and fumbled for the off switch on her radio alarm, then squinted at the digital clock. Six o'clock. She had fallen asleep around midnight, after reading the first couple pages of Irish's journal. It hadn't made much sense to her, but she knew that was because she'd been so upset and tired. She wanted to read it again, but this morning they were leaving for Eagle Lodge, and she wouldn't have time to do anything but last-minute packing.

She looked at the clock again, then reached for the telephone on her nightstand. Tia's parents had insisted she go to school today, so Kara knew she would be awake.

Tia picked up on the third ring. "What's up?"

Kara flinched. Her friend had gotten a telephone for Christmas, complete with caller ID. Kara wasn't sure she liked it, but that didn't matter now. "You aren't going to believe this, Tia, but remember the pages from my great-grandfather's journal? The ones that came with Irish's drawing?"

"Of the first Wakara? Sure, why?"

"They're bogus, Tia. A fake."

"What? You're kidding, right?"

Kara shook her head even though she knew her friend couldn't see. "I wish." Her throat tightened, and she swallowed back the tears. "I know it's stupid, but I feel betrayed; like Great-grandpa deliberately lied to me."

She went on to tell Tia about the journal and papers Grandpa Sheridan had found in the old trunk in Aunt Peg's garage. "I've only read the first few pages, but in his letter Grandpa says the journal entries prove the version on the other pages was a lie, and that Irish didn't want anyone to know about Wakara's true background. He says the motive is in the journal too, but he won't tell me any more. He says he wants me to read it and figure it out for myself, then maybe I'll understand."

"Wow! You're bringing it, aren't you? We can read it at the lodge."

Kara had to smile. Tia was the one who'd been there for her when she'd first discovered the name Wakara was not Nez Perce, as she'd always believed. Anne had insisted "Wakara" was a Yahi word meaning moon, and Tia had dug up research to prove her right. But knowing that had only deepened the mystery around her great-grandfather's words. Why had he told everyone the baby he'd found in the woods was Nez Perce, when he knew she wasn't? If he lied about that, how much of the rest was a lie?

"Earth to Wakara! I gotta go, Mom's rattling my cage to get ready for school, and I still have to finish packing for tomorrow. Bring the journal, okay?"

Kara sighed. "Don't worry, I will. Oh, I almost forgot. Grandpa still wants to read the paper you wrote on the Yahi-Yana tribes. He's still looking for something and thinks your research might hold the key—whatever that means. Could you mail it to him?"

"Are you kidding? I mailed it yesterday. It's halfway to Arizona by now."

By the time Kara got downstairs, Dad and Ryan were finishing breakfast. Dad studied her face. She must not look too upset, because he looked relieved, then smiled. "Good morning, Sugar Bear."

"Morning, Dad. What time is everyone leaving?"

Dad took a swallow of coffee and looked at his watch. "Soon. I still have to contact the ranger station, then file a flight plan. Shouldn't take long." He looked at Ryan. "You ready to go, Tiger?"

Ryan gulped down his orange juice and jumped up from the table. "Yeah. Kara helped me pack my bag last night. I'll go get it." He raced out of the room before Kara could tell him to slow down. She sighed, then realized Dad was looking at her again.

"Thanks, Wakara," he said. "I really appreciate all you do for Ryan."

Kara felt uncomfortable. She knew Dad was grateful for her help. He didn't have to keep telling her, but this morning it did feel good to hear him say something nice.

She helped herself to scrambled eggs and stuck a piece of bread in the toaster. When she sat down, Anne handed her a mug of coffee. "Thanks, Anne. Do you need any help?"

The cook shook her head. "No." Then she smiled. "It is only for one week."

Kara grinned back. "True. Wait until June." It was a lot more work getting ready to be away for three whole months. Last year, Anne hadn't been hired until they were already at Eagle Lodge. The supplies and gear had already been packed up and delivered by then.

Dad picked up his dishes and carried them to the sink, then turned toward the mud porch and lifted his jacket from a hook. "Bud Davis and Floyd Carlson will be here with

57

the stock trailers around ten o'clock. Greg and Colin should have the horses ready to go by then."

Kara felt a surge of excitement. The big stock trailer was on loan to another rancher who was taking an entire herd of cattle to auction. It would take two of the smaller trailers to transport six horses to the trailhead. Kara had actually ridden Dakota that distance last winter, but that was an emergency, and she wasn't eager to do it again. Instead, she and Greg and Colin would ride into the valley from Pine Creek Meadow. It wasn't an easy ride, but at least it was a trail.

"I'll get out there as soon as I'm finished," she promised as Dad opened the door.

He hesitated. "The boys will handle it. You see to your brother and help Anne. I'll let you know when we're ready to go."

Kara nearly dropped her fork. "What about Lily?"

"We'll handle it." He was gone before she could say anything else.

Kara sat there, stunned. She'd always helped with the horses, whether she was riding in or not. And Dad had just heard both Anne and Ryan say they were ready to go. No way did they need her help. "Anne?"

The cook was staring out the kitchen window, watching Dad walk to the barn. Kara jumped up and stood behind her. "Anne!" Kara knew her voice had risen about six octaves, but right now she didn't care. This time her eyes were dry; she was too scared and angry to cry.

"He is troubled." Anne turned from the window and put her arm around Wakara's shoulders.

"Why! What have I done?" She couldn't keep the fear and disappointment out of her voice. She felt like everyone was betraying her—even her own father—and that hurt so badly she could hardly stand it.

58

The woman led her to a chair, then sat beside her. Kara could tell she was uncomfortable, but if Anne knew what was going on . . .

"It is not what you have done that troubles him, but what could be."

Kara shook her head. "I don't get it."

Anne sighed and reached for Kara's hand. "In some cultures, a father sees a young man's feelings for his daughter and locks her away until the bride price has been paid."

Kara scowled. "What's that got to do with me?"

"In this culture, fifteen is young to be a bride. Your father does not realize it, but he is locking you away."

"Locking me away?" She shook her head. "I don't get it. I'm not even dating anyone. The only boys I ever see are Greg and Colin."

Anne said nothing, just squeezed her hand, and suddenly Kara understood.

"Colin?" She felt like her face was on fire. "But he's never . . . I mean I like him, but we've never even gone on a real date."

Anne smiled. "It is in the way he looks at you. Your father sees."

"And he's trying to keep me away from him." Kara felt a chill of anger. "That's not fair. Colin hasn't done anything wrong—he wouldn't, and neither would I. I thought Dad trusted me."

"A father's love is not always rational."

Kara looked up at her, astonished. "You mean he's punishing me because he loves me? Right!" She took a deep breath. *Get a grip, Wako, it's not Anne's fault.* Her throat grew tight, and she made herself choke back the tears. "That's just great; now what do I do? I wish Mom were here!"

The words were out before she knew she'd said them, but she realized they were true. If Mom were here, Dad wouldn't be acting like this.

"Yes."

Anne's voice was so soft Kara almost missed it. Then she blushed. "Oh, Anne, I'm sorry. Thank you for telling me. I was beginning to think Dad hated me, but I'm not sure this is any better."

"Shall I talk to him?"

Kara shook her head. "No. I guess I'd better do it. If he'll give me a chance."

The door slammed and Ryan rushed into the room, panting like he'd run a mile. "Kara, Anne, come on, the trucks are here and they're getting ready to load the horses."

Kara flinched. "I'll be right there, Ry." To her relief, he turned around and ran back into the yard.

She picked up her bag and was on the back porch before it hit her. *Colin likes me, and we're riding into the valley together!* That thought made her stomach flutter all the way to the barn.

The horses, including Lily, were already saddled and loaded into the trailers. Kara set her bag at the end of the walkway for Dad to take with him on the plane. Dad and Colin were standing by Mr. Carlson's truck, and Greg was already in the front passenger seat of Bud Davis's Land Rover. She headed for Mr. Davis's rig. No sense in making things worse by trying to squeeze into the truck with Colin.

"Wait a second, Wakara." She turned to see Dad walking toward her. "Here." He handed her a small paper bag. She opened it and held up a small canister that fit easily into the palm of her hand. "Pepper spray? What's this for?"

"When I talked to the ranger station, they told me there has been some problem with bears this spring," Dad answered. "Be sure and aim for the eyes. This packs a pretty good sting

60

and blinds them long enough for you to get out of the way."
She must have looked as nervous as she felt, because Dad laid
a hand on her shoulder. "I doubt you'll need it. Colin and
Greg each have one. Put Lily in the middle and stay with the
others. You shouldn't have any trouble."

Kara shivered. "I hope not. I've seen all the bears I want
to see for a while." On impulse she put her arms around
Dad and hugged him hard. He kissed the top of her head,
and when she moved away, he said, "Be careful, Sugar Bear.
Remember everything you've been taught and you'll be
fine."

She nodded and climbed into the backseat of the Land
Rover. It wasn't until they were almost to the end of the drive
that she realized Dad's words of caution could have a double meaning.

9

THE TRAIL WOUND DOWNWARD, SNAKELIKE, narrow, and steep for the first few miles. They had to ride single file, which didn't leave much opportunity to talk, but that was fine with Kara. She was still too confused about Colin's and her relationship, not to mention Dad's reaction to it. She knew by the way that Colin had been avoiding her that Dad had warned him off. The more she thought about it, the more it made her mad. Dad had probably insisted she ride in the middle not just to keep her safe, but so that she couldn't talk to Colin. He was in the lead and trailing another horse, which meant he could hardly turn around in the saddle to carry on a conversation. And Greg was bringing up the rear. Was he supposed to be the watchdog and keep an eye on them both?

She tried to distract her thoughts by studying the scenery. Most of the snow had melted, revealing a graveyard-like landscape with the skeletons of blackened trees scattered over acres of burned-out land. Where brush and wild rhododendrons once fought for space beneath the fir and juniper trees, a hint of green blanketed the damp, bare earth. When she looked closer, she could see tiny white wildflowers dotting the new grass like tie-knots on a hand-stitched quilt.

Kara took a deep breath of the clean spring air. *New growth—new life.* It was so amazing how quickly the earth was restored, even after something as devastating as a wildfire.

Colin pulled Dakota to a halt when they reached Otter Lake. The small basin was once again full of water from the melted snow, and Powell Creek ran fast, but shallow, dissecting the trail just below the lake. Colin stopped there to let the horses get a drink, then moved on across the creek. Kara let Lily drink her fill, then followed Colin to the other side.

"Are you watching this?" Colin tipped his hat back from his forehead and nodded toward the creek.

Kara heard Lyman snorting and Greg muttering under his breath as he tried to spur the skittish Arabian into the water. The horse behind them stood placidly, waiting for the lead mount to make up its mind. Kara tried not to laugh as Greg and his new horse wrestled it out. But Lyman was stubborn. Greg couldn't let go of the lead line, so he finally dismounted and led both animals across the creek.

"Keep it up and you're dog meat!" Greg slapped his hand against Lyman's rump, then remounted. The horse gave a little buck in protest. Greg stood in the stirrups, then plopped down hard into the saddle. The Arabian tossed his head once, then walked forward, placid as a little lamb.

Kara and Colin both gave in to laughter. Colin winked at her. "I'd call that a draw, wouldn't you?"

Kara shook her head. "I don't know. Something tells me Lyman thinks he's won."

"This time." There was a hint of a threat in her brother's tone, but he patted Lyman on the neck. "We've still got some work to do, don't we, boy?" He grinned at Colin and Kara. "All right, you guys, the rodeo is over. We've been at this for over three hours, and we're almost there. Let's get on with it."

Colin tipped his hat and turned Dakota down the trail. Kara sighed and fell in line. She had warned Greg that that horse would be a handful, but she could see how attached Greg had already become to him. It might take a lot of work to train Lyman, but Kara knew she would do the same as Greg.

When Eagle Lodge came into view thirty minutes later, they could see Dad's plane, with the brown-and-green logo on the side, still standing on the landing strip. The tractor was parked close to the tail section, where Anne and Ryan were pulling out luggage and hefting it into the small trailer for the quarter-mile trip uphill to the lodge. Ryan saw them coming and waved.

Kara watched as Ryan tried to wrestle a heavy duffel bag into the trailer. "Where's Dad?"

Anne looked up from her chore. "He is making repairs."

Ryan finally shoved the heavy bag over the side of the trailer. He wiped his hands down the legs of his jeans, then ran over to Greg and patted Lyman on the neck. Kara expected the horse to shy. Instead, he leaned into Ryan's hand like a contented pup.

"Dad's fixin' the door to the storage shed," Ryan told Greg. "It's all broke down, and I bet I know what did it." He lowered his voice to a mock whisper. "I'm not s'pose' to say in front of Kara, but there was claw marks all the way to the roof. Boy," he shook his head, "that must have been one big ol' bear."

Kara shivered and nudged Lily into a trot. When they got to the barn, she helped Greg and Colin unsaddle the horses. Lily and Dakota went eagerly into their stalls, but Lyman balked at the narrow entrance, so Greg led him to one of the outside stalls built along the back of the airplane hangar.

They were right off the corral, so Lyman still had the three other horses they had lead in for company. He sniffed out his new domain, then settled down to munch his pile of hay.

While Colin filled three five-gallon buckets with water and set them in the stalls, Kara filled the trough in the corral. The horses drank thirstily after the long ride, and Kara couldn't wait to quench her own thirst. "I hope Anne brought lemonade," she said as they took turns washing their hands under the water spigot. "I think I could drink a gallon by myself."

She followed the guys up the hill to Eagle Lodge and into the kitchen, where Anne had set out lemonade, bologna sandwiches, chips, and cookies. Kara ate her fill, then found Dad out behind the lodge. The door to the storage shed had been splintered down one side, and the frame was shredded beyond repair. Dad already had it sanded down and was adding strips of lumber for another frame.

"Whoa, that bear must have been starving."

Dad grunted in reply, then took a handful of nails out of his mouth. "It sure didn't take much in the way of food. Just destroyed the door. We'll have to buy a new one, but I doubt Mark has room to bring one tomorrow." He motioned her inside the shed. "You might want to help Anne out by taking this stuff into the kitchen. We'll have to keep all the food in there until I can finish the repairs."

Poor Dad, she thought as she filled a box with packages of pasta and dried beans. There was already so much to do around here, and this just added another chore to his list. They'd be lucky to get half of it done this week. She kept at it and managed to have all but the highest shelf cleared out by the time Anne called her in.

Dinner was spaghetti and salad Anne had brought from home. By nine o'clock, even Dad was yawning. "I don't know about the rest of you," he said, "but I'm ready for bed." His gaze traveled around the table. "Greg, you and Colin can bunk together, or one of you can take cabin number one."

Greg pulled a coin out of his pocket and tossed it to Colin. "Flip you for the cabin."

Colin grinned and shook his head. "Nah. You take it. I'm used to sleeping in small spaces. That closet was my bunk all last summer, remember?"

Dad nodded his approval, then said, "The flooring in my room is rotten in spots, so until we can get it fixed, I'll hole up in my office and Ryan can sleep upstairs. I set up a cot for him in Anne's room." Anne slipped an arm around Ryan, who yawned and leaned against her shoulder. "Wakara," Dad continued, "you can keep your usual room. When Tia gets here tomorrow she will bunk with you." Kara nodded. Her room was on the main floor of Eagle Lodge, across from Colin's and next to Ryan and Dad's. It was just as small as the others, but the floor was fine, and unlike Colin, she at least had a window.

When the dishes were done, Kara gathered up a towel and her shower sandals. The shower room was behind the lodge next to the storage shed. She hated going out there after dark, but unless she walked over to one of the cabins, there was no other choice.

She showered quickly without washing her hair and hurried back inside, bolting the door behind her. Dad had turned off the generator, so she used her flashlight to guide her through the kitchen and dining room. She turned left into the recreation room, careful not to bump into the pool table. She propped open the door to the hallway with a stack of jigsaw puzzles from the game shelf and tiptoed past Dad's door to her own room.

The room wasn't much bigger than a walk-in closet, but it housed a narrow bed and a small table that doubled as a desk. Wall shelves with pegs underneath held her books and clothes, and another small table under the narrow window held a lantern, water carafe, and glasses. Once she set up Tia's cot tomorrow, there wouldn't be much room to walk around, but they'd done it before and the arrangement had worked out fine. Kara stowed her flashlight on the table beside the bed, crawled under the covers, and fell instantly asleep.

A scraping sound like a tree branch rubbing against the window woke her. *The wind must be up,* she thought sleepily as she snuggled back under the covers. The scraping came again, this time followed by a thump and noises Kara couldn't identify.

She sat up in the thick, black darkness, suddenly realizing where she was. There weren't any trees even close to the windows here at Eagle Lodge. Dad kept the area around the buildings clear for more than thirty feet in case of fire. That's what had kept it from burning last summer.

She fumbled for her watch. The luminous dial read 2:00. Shivering, she pulled on her fur-lined slippers, grabbed her flashlight, and crept to the window. After pulling aside the curtains, she had full view of the meadow and two guest cabins with the woods beyond. The area between the lodge and cabin number one was bathed in the glow of a three-quarter moon. There in the middle of the clearing, a full-grown bear hunched over something on the ground.

Kara's stomach knotted in fear. She was tempted to go back to bed and pretend it wasn't there. But what if it didn't go away? Gulping down the lump that had formed in her throat, she slid open the window and shined the flashlight on the animal. "Hey!" she yelled at the top of her lungs. "Go on. Get out of here!"

The bear lifted its head toward the sound, and Kara gasped when she saw the thick, dark liquid that coated its face and dripped from its open jaws. She knew those jaws were capped with ugly yellowed teeth.

"Oh, gross!" The thought of some poor, defenseless little animal being ripped apart for the bear's dinner made her gag. She screamed, grabbed the water carafe from the table, and threw it as hard as she could. When the bear only grunted, she heaved the water glasses through the window. Yelling at the top of her lungs, she had just picked up the lantern when she heard the blast of a gunshot. She looked up to see Greg, dressed only in pajama bottoms, standing on the porch of cabin one. Her brother pointed his rifle into the air and fired a second time.

When she looked back, the bear had picked up whatever it had been chewing on and was lumbering as fast as it could toward the woods. Greg followed it with his gun, and for a heartbeat she thought he was going to shoot it, but the animal made the cover of the tree line, and her brother let it go.

If Dad knocked before shoving open her door, she didn't hear it over the sound of her own heartbeat thudding in her ears.

"Wakara!" He cringed from the glare of her flashlight, and she quickly turned it away.

"Sorry, Dad. You startled me."

"I startled you?" He strode to the window and pushed it shut. "You scared *me* out of three lives! What's going on in here?"

She started to explain about the bear, when Colin pushed into the room, followed by Greg. "Hey, Wakara, are you okay?" her brother asked. There was a chuckle in his voice.

She nodded, then realized he couldn't really see her. "I'm fine," she said.

Greg laughed. "Well, that bear's not. Between your screams and your pitching arm, I'd bet he's in Mexico by now."

Kara shivered in spite of her flannel pajamas. She hugged herself and sat down on the bed. "All he did was look at me.

He didn't take off until you fired those shots." She grinned at her brother. "Thanks, I owe you one."

Anne and Ryan were now standing in the doorway. With five flashlights pointed into the room, she saw Greg's mouth spread into a huge grin. "I'd call it even," he said, and she felt a rush of love for her older brother.

Dad cleared his throat and gestured to the crush of bodies in the room. "All right, everybody out. I'll call the ranger station in the morning and report a rogue bear. In the meantime, we all need to get some sleep."

Greg and Colin moved to leave, but not before Kara saw the look that flashed between them. They would track the animal at the first hint of light. Should she say anything to Dad?

He didn't give her a chance. "Wakara, I want you upstairs with Anne."

"What? Dad, you can't be serious! Why?"

He ran one hand through his hair, and she thought for a minute he was going to back down. Instead he said, "Just do it, Wakara. I'm too tired to argue."

She started to protest again, but from the look on his face she knew it wouldn't do any good. He was treating her like a two-year-old. *How embarrassing!* Fighting back tears of frustration, she grabbed her pillow and followed Anne up the stairs.

When Kara woke the room was still dark, but Anne was already up. Kara knew the woman would be either in the kitchen or outside in some quiet place, reading her Bible and praying. Mom had done the same thing. Every morning without fail, Kara would find her in the kitchen or family room with her Bible and an open notebook with a list of people to pray for.

Kara felt a stab of guilt. *How old were Mom and Anne when they started doing that?* Her own Bible was still on the desk in her room at home. *I pray every day,* she reminded herself. *And go to church on Sunday. Youth group too.* But sometimes that didn't seem to be enough. Especially when things in her life seemed to be going sideways, like now.

She got up and moved to the window, careful not to wake Ryan, who was still curled up on his cot with his head buried underneath the covers.

The sky was just beginning to lighten above the gray morning mist. Something stirred in the shadows, then moved into the clearing where the bear had been the night before. Kara rubbed a clear spot on the frosty glass and peered closer. *Colin and Greg!* They were studying something on the ground, and both of them carried rifles. Just as she thought, they were going after that bear.

Tendrils of smoke snaked upward into an ice blue sky. The smell of burning cedar told her Anne had lit a log in the fireplace as well as the woodstove in the kitchen. Kara shivered. The room was cold enough to see her breath. Quickly she stuffed her feet into her slippers, grabbed her pillow, and hurried downstairs.

10

BACK IN HER OWN BEDROOM, Kara pulled on jeans and a sweatshirt with a picture of a kitten hanging from a tree branch by its claws. The caption read "Hang in There." *Exactly the advice I need,* she thought. She had to have a talk with Dad, and it had to be soon. Once Tia arrived, opportunities for privacy would be zero.

The lodge was quiet except for the crackle of flames licking at a huge log in the dining-room fireplace. The fire gave the room a cozy, warm glow, and Kara eyed the two small, overstuffed chairs that flanked the hearth. *Coffee first, then one of those is mine!* She loved it here at Eagle Lodge, especially the quiet moments when no one else was around. The front wall of the dining room was practically one big window that offered an unbroken view of meadows, the river, and the mountains beyond.

No one was in the kitchen, but the back door was ajar, and Kara knew Anne wasn't very far away. She grabbed a mug from the rack by the ancient percolator and poured herself a cup of the steaming brew. She turned to head back to the fireplace, but stopped when she heard a voice com-

71

ing from the radio room. Ryan loved to play in there even though it was strictly forbidden. Had he awakened and come down while she was in her room?

She hurried to the door, which was open just a crack, and peeked in. The last thing she wanted to do was scare him into dropping the controls like he had the last time. That had been an expensive lesson and could have cost them their lives.

Instead of Ryan, Kara realized it was Dad sitting in the radio room with his back to her. He was talking to someone on the radio. She was about to turn away when Dad said, "Right. Tell Mark not to bring Tia. He'll have three passengers going home instead."

Kara braced herself against the table. Not bring Tia? And who was going home? He had to mean her and Ryan and probably Anne. *How could he do this! And for absolutely no reason!*

A few seconds later, Dad confirmed her fears. "Sorry, Wakara," he said when he saw her in the kitchen. "I know you won't like it, but it's just not safe here right now. Once a bear has become a nuisance, they seldom go away on their own. You know that." He didn't give her a chance to get a word in edgewise. "The ranger station is sending a crew to tranquilize and relocate this animal, but they can't get to it until tomorrow at the earliest. I'd prefer not to have to worry about you and Tia and Ryan getting in its way."

Kara swallowed back her anger. A shouting match would only make things worse and prove she was as immature as Dad was treating her. She hadn't heard Anne come in, but the cook stood at the counter cracking eggs into a bowl. Kara looked at Anne, hoping for some backup and once again wishing Mom were here to take her side. But Mom wasn't here, and Anne had no control over Dad. He was her boss.

Dad was already turning toward the door. "Dad, wait!" Kara jumped up and stepped in front of him. "I need to talk to you."

He scowled. "Now?" He glanced at Anne, and Kara wondered if he, too, wanted someone on his side. "This really isn't a good time, Wakara. Anne's making breakfast."

Kara refused to give up. "Please, Dad, it's important."

"Breakfast will keep, a daughter will not," Anne said quietly.

Kara stood perfectly still. *Yes! Thank you, Anne!*

Dad's eyes widened in shock, and then his shoulders drooped like he'd just had the wind knocked out of him. Kara bit her lower lip to keep herself quiet. The few seconds it took Dad to decide seemed like an hour. Finally, he exhaled slowly and flashed her a defeated grin.

"All right, might as well get it over with," he said. "Want to go outside?"

Kara nodded. She followed him to the front door, grabbed her jacket off the rack, and joined him at the far end of the deck. Dad sat down on the bench and patted the seat next to him, but she pulled up a chair so that she was facing him. *God,* she prayed quietly, *in the Bible You promised You'd give us words to say when we need them. This may not be exactly what You meant, but I sure need the right words now. Please!*

She looked Dad in the eyes. "You've always told me how mature and responsible I am and how much you depend on me. Until a few days ago, I thought you trusted me." She took a deep breath and tried to keep her voice from shaking. "I need to know what I've done to lose your trust."

Dad looked startled. "Nothing!" He shook his head, "I mean, it has nothing to do with trust, Wakara." He reached over and took her hand. "I still think you are mature for your age, and you've certainly proved you're responsible, even if you did take a big risk by riding Lily without a helmet." He squeezed her hand. "But I have to tell you, Sweet-heart, that episode with the bear back in Lariat really shook me. You could have been killed! And quite honestly, I don't think I could live with that."

Especially after losing Mom. He hadn't said that, but she knew that was part of it.

"Now we've got this nuisance bear on our hands," he continued, "and, frankly, I can't take the risk of you or your brother getting hurt. And," he silenced her by holding up one finger, "that goes double when it comes to being responsible for someone else's child like Tia." He ran one hand through his hair. "I really think it's best for Mark to take you guys and Anne home."

Kara wanted to scream "Foul!" But instead of arguing, she decided to try and be reasonable. "Look, Dad, when did you say the rangers were coming to relocate this pest?"

"Tomorrow afternoon. Maybe as late as Monday morning. That is, assuming they can track him and pin him down."

"Just listen, okay?" Dad looked at the sky with a give-me-patience attitude, but he nodded yes, and Kara went on. "I know how much work there is to do around here, and we both know Tia and I can do almost as much of it as the guys. What if we promise to keep Ry with us and work right along-side you? We can save the other stuff like clearing trails and scouting the river for later, after they take care of that bear."

Dad shook his head, but she saw his mouth quirk sarcastically. "There's more than one bear in the woods, Wakara."

"There's always been more than one bear in the woods," she reminded him. "This year is no different than last year and the year before. Tia and I won't go anywhere alone, I promise. And I won't let Ryan out of my sight. He'll be with us or with Anne at all times."

Dad blew out a long breath, and Kara held hers. Finally, after what seemed like an eternity, he threw up his hands.

"All right. I must be out of my mind, but Tia can come and you can stay—if you promise to stay close to the house and other people at all times. Clear?"

Kara sighed and nodded. "Clear."

"Good. Now, can we eat? I'm starved."

Kara hesitated. She hadn't expected to have to deal with the safety issue. She had really wanted to talk about her and Colin. But Dad's face was pale, and he looked like he just might be out of patience. *Better not push it,* she decided.

"Hey, Wakara! Hold up, we've got something for you."

She shielded her eyes with one hand against the morning sun and waited for Greg and Colin to leap onto the porch. Colin held something behind his back, and she didn't like the hint of mischief in Greg's smile.

Without thinking, she backed up a step. "What is it?" She was glad to see that Dad had stopped at the front door and turned around.

"Where have you two been?" He scowled at the boys, but Greg just grinned.

"Tracking bear," he said. "We didn't find him, but we did find the 'animal' he was chewing on when Kara tried to brain him with the water pot."

Gross! Kara felt like she might throw up, but no way was she going to give Greg the satisfaction! Not to mention how embarrassing that would be in front of Colin. She clenched her fists and faced the guys head-on. "All right, what is it? A rabbit or a dead squirrel?"

Greg and Colin looked at each other and burst out laughing as Colin thrust something cold and sticky into her hands. "Salsa!" they yelled in unison.

Kara almost dropped the disgusting mess, but then she realized they were right. "Dad, look, it is salsa! An entire plastic gallon jug." She looked at her brother and Colin, who were practically rolling on the ground with laughter.

Kara started laughing too. "You mean he ate this? The whole thing?" Then she remembered the top shelf in the storage shed. She couldn't reach it and had meant to take the kitchen stool out after dinner last night, but she'd forgotten all about it.

"I don't know about you," Greg said, gasping for breath, "but I wouldn't want to be anywhere near that critter right about now."

"Me either," Colin howled. "Especially not downwind!"

After breakfast, Dad managed to contact Mark before he could call Tia and tell her the trip was off. They arrived shortly after 12:30. Anne fed everyone lunch, and Dad declared an hour's reprieve before afternoon chores. He had also relented and allowed them to stay in Kara's room.

"Colin and Greg spent the rest of the morning making up silly poems about salsa-slurping bears," Kara told Tia as they set up her bed. "I think the mountain air has fried their brains."

Tia laughed. "For them, that's normal!" She shoved her backpack underneath her cot and squirmed around for a more comfortable position. "Anyway, I'm glad you convinced your dad to let us stay! I already cancelled a zillion plans."

"You know we have to work," Kara reminded her. "You might wish you had stayed home."

"What, and miss a week with the most exciting family in the universe? Not a chance!" She glanced around the tiny room. "Anyway, this will give us a chance to read your great-grandfather's journal. The real one, I mean. Where is it?"

Kara pulled the cardboard notebook out from under her pillow. "Here. And look, there's pages ripped out from the back."

Tia frowned. "Huh? Weird. Like, maybe he decided he didn't want anyone to read them."

Kara shook her head. "No. I think those pages are the *only* ones he wanted people to read." She pulled out the two sheets of paper that her Great-grandfather Sheridan had taped to the back of her great-grandmother's picture. "Look at the paper—the jagged ends match almost perfectly."

"Wow!" Tia's scowl deepened. "I don't get it. Why would he rip out just two pages and put them with the picture? Didn't you say he gave them to your Grandpa Sheridan himself?"

Kara rolled her eyes. "Don't you see? These two pages tell the story Great-grandpa wanted people to believe. I've only read a little, but from what Grandpa said, the rest of the journal proves this version is a lie."

"Why?" Tia howled. "I don't get it. What difference did it make how he found her?" She reached for the journal. "More important, what's the real story? I can't wait to read it!"

Kara pulled the journal out of reach and stuffed it under her pillow. "Neither can I, but I haven't had a chance to get very far." She looked at her watch. "And we don't have time now, either. Dad said to meet him at the barn by two o'clock. We're supposed to wear work boots and heavy gloves."

A thud against her bedroom door proved her right. "Hey, Kara!" Ryan yelled. "You in there? I'm supposed to tell you two it's time to get to work, and you have to take me with you—Dad said!"

Dad was waiting at the barn with shovels, a manure rake, and two wheelbarrows. "I put Lily in the corral with the others so she could get some fresh air and be out of the way. Greg and Colin rode out on Lyman and Dakota to fix any breaks in the pasture fence." He led the way into the old building. "We shored up that back wall and it held through the winter, but we need to restore and seal all the walls or the whole place is going to collapse. Before we can do that, it needs to be cleaned out."

"Why not just build a new barn, Mr. S.?" Tia asked.

Dad shook his head. "Too expensive. And there's really no need. Whoever built this barn used entire trees for posts and beams, and we put a new roof on it right after we bought the place." He swept his arm around the cavernous room. "Because of the equipment shed, we really don't need this much storage down here. I'd like to rebuild the stalls, but that will have to wait a year or two." He sighed and handed Ryan a short, flat shovel.

"Ryan, you muck the stalls while Wakara and Tia clear out some of this mess." He pointed to one corner. "Put anything still usable over there. The rest goes to the junk pile. I've got someone coming to haul it out of here at the end of the week. When you get to the floor, use the shovels. We'll fix any dry rot when we come back in June."

Kara groaned, and Tia made a face. Dad just grinned and headed for the door. "I'll be working on the corral. Oh, and girls?"

"Yes, Dad?"

"Be careful of spiders, now, you hear?"

"Spiders!" Tia squealed, and Kara could hear Dad laughing all the way to the corral.

11

"WELL, WE DID IT," Kara moaned when she and Tia finally got back to her room. "I may never move a muscle again, but the barn is clean!"

Tia stretched out on the bed and breathed a contented sigh. "It's miraculous," she said. "A hundred years' worth of dirt and junk, and we dug it out in four hours."

Kara winced and bent from the waist to stretch out her back. "There was no miracle involved, Tia Sanchez. We did it with the muscle God gave us." She eased herself onto the bed and propped the pillow so she could see her friend. "I wish we had some of Anne's juniper oil. But there's no place to soak."

Tia nodded. "Not a bathtub in sight."

Kara laughed. "If there were, we'd have to stand in line. Everyone worked hard today."

Tia grinned. "Yeah, everyone but Ryan. Did you see your little brother? Greg better watch out or he's going to lose a horse."

Kara relaxed back onto her pillow. "You mean Lyman?"

"Sure. Ryan cleaned the stalls in the barn, then headed straight for the corral. Did you notice he didn't leave that horse's side all day?"

Kara frowned. Tia was right. Ryan had spent most of the afternoon brushing Lyman and feeding him apple treats. She remembered thinking it really wasn't safe for him to be handling the spirited Arabian by himself, but Dad was right there, and he didn't seem worried. "You're right," she finally said. "I think maybe my little brother has outgrown his pony and is ready for a real horse. Not Lyman though." She yawned and closed her eyes. "Maybe an older mare. Doesn't Mrs. Bryant have one for sale?"

Her answer came in the form of a soft snore from the other bed. Kara propped herself on one elbow. Sure enough, Tia was out. Kara yawned again, reached over, and turned off the lantern. "I'm really blessed, aren't I, God? You've given me a great family and neat friends."

A picture of Colin flashed behind her closed eyes. Colin leaning against the porch railing, staring up into the heavens with that Cheshire Cat grin. She fell asleep with a smile on her face.

"Wakara! Wakara, wake up!"

A hand was shaking her. At first she tried to ignore it, but the urgency in the voice drew her up through the mire of a deep, dreamless sleep. Her mind felt like it was wrapped in a thick cotton batting, and she had to concentrate to understand the words.

"Wakara, listen, something's spooking the horses. Bad!"

The terror in Tia's tone finally brought Kara fully awake. "What?" she said groggily. "Horses? Tia, what are you . . . ?"

"Shh. Listen!"

She heard it then. A sound like thunder, stomping hooves and shrill whinnies, then the unmistakable scream of an animal in pain. A chill spread down her arms into her back and legs.

Men's voices and the sound of a shotgun blast spurred her into action. "The horses! Tia, grab a flashlight." She struggled into her flannel shirt and pulled on her boots.

This can't be happening, she thought, *not again!* Just last June, a bear had broken into the barn and raided the sacks of grain. Greg and Colin had scared him off before he went near the horses, but he'd broken through the corral and spooked the whole herd. This time it sounded like things were worse. *Much worse!* she thought as a horse screamed again. Another gunshot sent her adrenaline into overdrive. Fighting off panic, she jumped to her feet and raced out the door.

Colin met her at the bottom of the steps. His face was white, and in spite of the cold night air, his forehead was dripping sweat. "Wakara, wait," he panted. "Let me catch my breath." Hands on hips, he straightened his back and drew in a lungful of air.

Tia ran up behind her as Colin continued, "We need a blanket and some old sheets if you can find some. That blasted bear was back, and he took a swipe at Lyman. It's hard to tell with just a flashlight, but it looks like he ripped out a pretty good chunk of hide. The first aid kit won't be enough."

"I'll tell Anne." Tia ran back into the house. A few seconds later, Anne appeared with a stack of sheets and an old wool army blanket. Kara grabbed them and started down the steps, then heard Tia yell, "Ryan, come back here!"

"You let go of me!" the boy yelled. "I got to help Lyman!"

"Ry, wait!" Kara tried to grab him, but her arms were full of linens, and she missed as he shot by her like a bullet from a high-powered rifle. *Give me strength.* She breathed the prayer, then raced down the hill after him.

Kara was used to doctoring the horses. She'd always wanted to be a vet, and blood didn't upset her, but suffering did. She cringed as Lyman screamed again, then the generator roared to life and the corral was flooded with light. When she stopped to catch her breath, what she saw sent a chill of fear up her spine. Even as she hurried forward to help, her brain registered the scene in fragments, gathering information and storing it like a computer into useful bites. Lyman on the ground, blood gushing from a gaping wound on his hip. Dad trying to hold the wound together with his bare hands. Greg at his horse's head, trying to calm him. Colin laying across Lyman's body, helping Dad hold the wound closed and keeping the struggling horse penned down.

"Ryan, get back!" Greg's voice rang sharp and angry as he pushed their little brother away. "Go on, now. You'll just make things worse."

"No, I won't!" Ryan yelled, then his voice softened as he approached the horse. Staying just out of Greg's reach, he crooned, "Lyman needs me, don't you, boy?" He knelt and began to stroke the frantic animal on the neck, rubbing his hands under the mane and down the shoulder.

As Kara knelt next to Dad, the horse gave a great sigh and lay still. "Is he dead?" She pressed two fingers against the facial artery along the edge of his jawbone and felt a strong, fast pulse.

"No." Greg's tone was still sharp, but he quit trying to push Ryan away.

Thank you, God, she thought and began to examine the now quiet animal. *Vital signs first.* Her brain ticked off the things she had learned. *He's breathing, and the heart rate is fast but strong. But he's bleeding heavily and could go into shock.* Colin helped her cover the animal with the blanket. Dad gave up his hold on the wound. Blood seeped out of an inch-deep gash along the hip and thigh and oozed from deep scratches all the way down to the hock.

It seeped and oozed, but it didn't spurt. "Not an artery." Kara breathed a sigh of relief. "And it's bleeding enough that we won't need to flush it." She folded one of the sheets to make a thick pad and set it gently over the wound. Dad immediately used both hands to apply pressure, while Kara examined the more superficial scratches farther down on Lyman's leg. The horse flinched at her touch. "Do we have any Betadine?"

"Getting it now," Colin said, and she realized he had moved off of the horse and was digging through the first aid kit. In just a few seconds, he handed her the bottle of antiseptic and a sterile sponge. "Keep petting him, Ryan," she said. "This might sting a little."

The little boy nodded and did what he was told, but his hands were shaking. Kara noticed that he kept his back to her so he couldn't see the wounds. Lyman struggled a bit, then gave up and lay still. In a few seconds she had cleaned the scratches, and Colin handed her another sponge and a jar of Furicine.

"Trade," she said, and passed him the second sheet. "You and Greg tear this into several strips. Try and keep it off the ground so it doesn't get dirty." Greg and Colin stood and began tearing up the sheet, keeping it stretched between them, while Kara carefully applied the soothing antibiotic gel, then took the first long strip and bound it around the horse's leg. She wiped sweat from her forehead with the sleeve of her flannel shirt and glanced at Dad. His head was bent; his eyes focused on what he was doing. Kara felt a stab of frustration as she saw blood already seeping through the sheet. *What now?* "We can't elevate it," she said aloud. "He's too heavy to move, and I hate to jostle the wound."

"We have to bind it at least," Dad's voice sounded raspy. "My arms are giving out."

"We can do it," Colin and Greg said together.

Kara nodded. "Okay, we'll try, but first we'll need some towels to make a thicker pad."

"They are here."

Kara turned and saw Anne behind her. "Whoa. Anne, thanks, that's perfect." She accepted two thick, white towels and immediately set them on top of the blood-soaked sheet.

Dad resumed pressure until Colin and Greg were ready with several long strips of sheet, then he said, "Let's do this fast. I'll help Colin lift while Kara shoves these under his hip. Greg, you lay across his neck and shoulders just in case. Ryan, if this horse tries to get up, I want you away from him fast, understood?"

The back of Ryan's head bent in what looked like a nod, but Kara was afraid that if it came down to it, he wouldn't move fast enough. *Please, God,* she breathed a silent prayer, then smiled as Anne joined Ryan by the horse's head. Anne began a soft crooning song, adding her touch to Ryan's. Lyman relaxed, and in seconds the strips were under the horse's rump. Dad placed his hands over the towels and pressed down once again, while Kara tied the fabric straps tightly over the wound, making a pressure bandage.

When she was done, Dad sat flat on the ground with a groan of relief. Anne's hands reappeared, offering three large bags of frozen peas. Kara almost laughed. "Anne, you're a genius," she said as they placed the flexible ice packs around the padded wound.

"Mister Sheridan?" Tia's voice called from outside the circle of light. "The vet is on the radio and wants to talk to you."

Dad jumped to his feet and hurried to the water spigot to wash off his hands. Kara moved the ice packs just enough to peek at the edges of the towels. They were still white, and she breathed a sigh of relief. "You can tell him I think the bleeding has stopped, or slowed way down, anyway." She felt the side of Lyman's neck. "His pulse is strong, and his heart rate has slowed down quite a bit too. Oh, and tell him I don't think there are any tendons involved, but he's going to need stitches, lots of them." *And please, Lord, let him get here quick. I don't want to be the one to do it!*

Dad paused beside her and laid his hand against her cheek, then his fingers slid down and tipped her chin back until she could see his face. "Good job, Wakara. I mean that. We couldn't have done it without you." His gaze shifted from her to where Colin and Greg had collapsed on the ground, then to Anne and Ryan, who still sat rubbing the horse's neck. "You were troopers, all of you, and Lyman is going to be fine!"

After Dad had joined Tia for the trek up the hill to the lodge, Ryan turned to her and whispered, "Is he, Kara? Is Lyman really going to be okay?"

His face was pale, and tears were coursing in rivulets down his cheeks. She wanted to pull him close and hold him, like she had that evening after they had escaped from the fire and he had been so scared that she was going to die. She started to reach for him, but saw her hands were still wet with Lyman's blood, so she hid them in her lap.

"Yes, Ry. Lyman's going to live. And you really helped calm him down. I'm proud of you."

She looked over at Greg, who nodded. "Yeah, so am I," he said. "Thanks, Tiger. It's obvious Lyman trusts you."

"'Course he does. That's 'cuz I love him, lots." Ryan swiped at his eyes with the back of his hand and let Anne help him to his feet.

Greg's gaze followed them as Anne led Ryan away. "Maybe Lyman has the wrong owner."

Greg's tone wasn't bitter, just thoughtful, but Kara's head snapped up. "Don't even go there! Lyman is way too much horse for Ryan," she insisted.

Greg's eyes challenged her. "I don't know about that. You haven't seen them work together. Ryan gets a lot more cooperation out of him than I do." He leaned forward and with his fingers brushed the forelock between Lyman's ears.

Two hours later Mark's plane arrived, and the vet took over Lyman's care. After his examination, he turned to Kara and echoed Dad's praise. "Well done, young lady. Your Dad says you want to be a vet." Kara nodded, and he continued, "Well, when you get ready to do your internship, you've got a job with me."

She looked at him, astounded. *Close your mouth, Wakara, or you might catch a fly.* Mom's teasing voice sounded in Kara's ears.

"And to show you I'm not just spouting air, how would you like to help me stitch this thing shut?"

12

AT BREAKFAST, KARA COULD HARDLY keep her eyes open. Anne had fixed scrambled eggs and ham for the family, as well as for Mark, the vet, and a forest ranger who had come along to evaluate the bear situation. The ranger's name was Brad. *Probably twenty-five,* Kara guessed, *and drop-dead gorgeous!* She made an effort to concentrate on her breakfast. Tia was doing her best to embarrass both of them; practically drooling over the guy. If Tia hadn't been down at the other end of the table, Kara would have kicked her in the shin.

"We'll get that bear," Greg was saying. "Colin and I followed his tracks yesterday morning, so we know which direction he goes, even if the trail's cold."

Brad took a swallow of coffee, then set the mug carefully on the table. By the look on his face, Kara knew he was thinking about his answer. He wiped his mouth with a napkin, then looked at Greg. "I think it would be better if you guys get some rest and let the forest service handle it."

"When? You said yourself no one else is coming until tomorrow. Are we supposed to just sit back and let that bear chew up the entire herd?"

Kara could tell Greg was getting hot, and evidently so could Dad. He leaned over and placed a hand over Greg's arm. "That's enough, Son."

"It sure is!" Greg's tone was bitter. He pushed away from the table and started to stomp off, but Brad's voice stopped him.

"Listen up, Greg." Greg turned around. His face was red with anger, and his eyes were puffy from lack of sleep. Kara felt a rush of pity for her brother. Lyman was the best thing that had happened to him in the last couple of years. She could understand how upset he was, not to mention exhausted.

"Look," Brad's tone softened when he had Greg's attention. "I don't blame you for wanting that bear dead. But like it or not, it's against the law for you to shoot it. We have enough trouble with poachers doing that. I'll be back tomorrow with a team and my tracking dog. We'll dart the bear and relocate it somewhere the other side of Cedar Ridge."

Colin pushed his plate away and got to his feet. "We'll take turns keeping watch tonight. I can't imagine him coming back, but if he does, we can scare him off."

Brad nodded. "You do that. But if I get back here and find out that that bear's been shot, it better be in your cabin with its jaws wrapped around someone's leg. Clear?"

Colin and Greg looked at each other. Colin nodded once, then followed Greg out of the room.

Mark cleared his throat. "Well, I don't know about the rest of you, but I've got to get back to work. Doctor, Brad, if you're finished here, I think we'd better take off."

The men thanked Anne for breakfast and shook hands with Dad. "Your daughter will make a good vet some day, Harley." The doctor winked at Kara. "She's got my instructions for taking care of that horse. I didn't see anything to

88

indicate any lasting damage. Just keep him isolated for a few days, and he should be right as rain in a couple of weeks."

Kara and Tia helped Anne with the morning chores, then headed for their room. It was only a little after noon, but they'd been awake since 2:00 A.M., and Kara could hardly hold her head up.

"I don't know about you," Tia moaned, "but I'm going to sleep for a year."

"Make that two years!" Kara peeked out the window. The shades in cabin number one were drawn, and her brother's jacket was hanging on a rack outside the door. She yawned, crawled into bed, and closed her eyes.

It was dark again when Kara awoke and went down to check on Lyman. The generator was silent, and Greg sat in the dark, propped against the stall door with his rifle in his hand. When she walked up, the three packhorses trotted off to the other side of the corral.

"They're still a little nervous," Greg said.

Kara nodded. "I can see why." She shined her flashlight into the darkened stall where Lyman stood head down, eyes closed, apparently asleep. "How is he?" she asked Greg.

"He's doing okay. Dad brought Ryan down an hour ago with a couple of apple cores. Lyman gobbled them up. The wound looks nasty, but clean."

Kara nodded. "That's good. The vet said he could have some Banamine whenever he needs it." She yawned. "I'm going to check on Lily and Dakota. Is Colin going to relieve you?"

"Yeah." Greg pulled the horse blanket he was wrapped in closer around his shoulders. "He already fed the others. They're put up for the night."

A quick check of the old barn showed that Greg was right. Lily and Dakota were quietly munching their ration of hay.

Lily nickered and bumped Kara affectionately, then went back to her meal.

Kara trudged up the hill to the lodge, where Anne had set out cold cuts and bread. Tia ate a sandwich, yawned hugely, and headed back to bed. Kara took a few bites, swallowed some orange juice, and joined her friend.

They woke on Monday morning to the clatter of helicopter blades. Kara pulled on a sweat suit and hurried outside to the front deck. From there she could see all the way to the river and the meadow, where a huge forest service helicopter had just touched down. Tia joined her just as Mark's plane landed. It taxied over the bumpy ground and came to a stop just outside the hangar, where Dad's plane was tied down for the week. A man and a dog climbed down over the wing and headed to the spot where the chopper had landed.

The screen door slammed and Ryan charged out of the house, one arm in his jacket sleeve and the other sleeve dangling out of reach behind him. "Hey, Brad's back," he yelled as he bolted from the porch before Kara could help him.

"I'm out of here," Tia squealed as she ran her hands through her tangled hair and ducked out of sight.

Kara laughed. "You're right. If we don't get cleaned up, they'll sick the dog on us!"

By the time she and Tia finished washing, dressing, and brushing their teeth, the men were gathered in the dining room. Anne was just coming through the kitchen door with a huge platter of pancakes. The three rangers, including Brad, stood and nodded a greeting, while Mark squeezed Kara's shoulders in an affectionate hug. "Morning, Princess. Ready to catch a bear?"

Kara grinned back at him. "Not on your life. For once I'm happy to leave that to the experts."

Brad smiled and used a hand signal, which brought the dog lying at his feet to a sitting position. "Then you should meet the expert," he said. "Ladies, may I present Beaker, the best bear dog in the state of Oregon."

One of the other rangers chuckled. "You mean the only bear dog in the state of Oregon."

Kara reached out her hand. The black-and-white dog sniffed it, let out a short, sharp bark, and then lifted his paw for her to shake. "Is he a Husky?"

"He's a Karelian." Brad patted the dog, then lowered his hand, and the animal once again lay down at his feet.

"He's really friendly, Kara," Ryan said around a mouthful of pancakes. "Brad let me pet him before, and he likes me."

"What's a Karelian?" Tia avoided the dog and slid into the empty seat on the other side of Brad, not taking her eyes off his face. Kara rolled her eyes and sat down next to Dad.

If Brad was embarrassed by Tia's attention, he didn't show it. "A Karelian is a special breed," he explained. "They're superintelligent and have been trained to work a bear on the ground, like a cow dog would round up a stray. A hound will tree a bear, then the hunter shoots it, or in our case, darts it with a tranquilizer gun. This dog rushes in for a nip, then backs off. He can move like lightning from every direction and hold a bear in one spot until we can get a dart into him." He paused and looked at Dad. "Relocation is really not the best way; you need to know that. A bear is territorial, and given a chance, will usually return to its home territory."

Dad frowned. "What other choice do we have?"

Brad shook his head. "None." Kara could hear the frustration in his voice. "If I had another dog, more men, and a couple of weeks, we'd have that bear totally trained to stay away from people."

Greg grunted. "What about horses?"

Kara had to admire Brad for keeping his cool. "Horses too. This is a black bear we're dealing with here, folks, not a grizzly. Black bears rarely attack a human, and you notice he only took a swipe at your horse. A grizzly would have chewed it to pieces." He shook his head. "This guy's being a nuisance because he's hungry. It was a hard winter, and after the fire last summer, food is scarce."

"I'm sympathetic to that," Dad said, "but we don't have a couple of weeks. We're here until next Sunday, then we won't be back until the first of June. I can't risk that animal coming in here and wrecking the place. And," he gestured to Colin and Greg, "I can't spare the manpower to guard the stock every night."

Brad nodded. "Fair enough. We'll nab the animal and release him the other side of Cedar Ridge. If we're lucky, it might take him until August to work his way back. By then his belly will be full, and he'll be less inclined to be around humans." He looked pointedly at Greg. "Or horses."

The rangers thanked Anne for the breakfast and headed out the door, Beaker following obediently at Brad's heel. His tail was going a hundred miles an hour, and Kara could see the muscles quiver up and down his back. Did he know he was going on a hunt? *Dogs sense those things,* she thought as she poured syrup over another pancake.

"I wish they'd let me go," Ryan whined. "I could help." He brightened. "It would be an adventure. Like the Crocodile Hunter, only with bears!"

Everyone laughed, and Mark spoke up. "Speaking of adventures, I guess the youth group had quite a rafting trip." Kara felt a stab of envy and quickly pushed it aside.

Colin's head snapped up. "Oh yeah? What happened? How did it go?"

"It went fine," Mark chuckled, "until Mr. Andrews steered to the wrong side of Donner's Rock and dumped the whole raftload of kids into the water. Luckily everyone was wearing life jackets, and the current pushed them toward shore.

Mr. Andrews stayed with the boat and came out about a mile ahead. He was one scared man until he hiked back and found all the others safe and sound."

"Did they finish the run?" Colin asked.

"Sure. I guess a couple of the parents were upset because the kids were an hour late getting back to home base, but when Mr. Andrews explained, they were just relieved that no one was injured."

"Man, would I love to get my raft in the water," said Colin. Kara's heart raced at the gleam of excitement in his eyes. "Brad said the water level is perfect right now. In another week or so, it'll be too high." He glanced at Greg.

They're up to something, Kara thought when she saw the look that passed between them.

Sure enough, Greg set down his juice glass and cleared his throat. "Uh, Dad?" Dad's fork paused halfway to his mouth at the tone of Greg's voice. Kara held back a giggle. Greg was so obvious!

"Remember when we were talking about adding white-water rafting to the activities at Eagle Lodge?" He went on before Dad could say anything. "Colin and I were thinking we might make a trial run this weekend, test out the raft and check out the rapids. Assuming, of course, all the repairs are done by Thursday night. We could leave Friday morning and be back by Saturday night in time to help close up the lodge."

Everyone at the table was staring at Dad except for Anne, who bowed her head over her plate, Kara assumed to hide her smile. After a few seconds of silence, Dad said seriously, "What makes you think we'll get everything done by Friday? We haven't exactly had the best start."

"I'm pretty sure we can handle it, Mr. Sheridan," Colin said. "And white-water rafting or fishing excursions would sure bring in extra income. I took the Stewarts out in the old raft last season, and they loved it. The new one is bigger and will hold more people. But," he went on, sounding even more eager than Greg, "there's no way we can take the public out without checking the course of the river first. Between the fire and the heavy snow, things could have changed a lot."

"He's right, Mr. S.," Tia piped up. "Wakara and I will help get stuff done. Four in the boat will make it like a real run." She flashed Colin a brilliant smile.

Way to go, Tia! Kara held her breath. Would Dad go along with this? *Oh, please, please, please!* She wanted to jump up and down and beg like a puppy, but that was definitely not the way to get around Dad. Besides, she could tell by the scowl on Greg's face that he really hadn't meant for her and Tia to go. But Colin just returned Tia's grin. He fiddled with his fork, and Kara could tell he was doing his best to act casual while waiting for Dad's answer.

She held her breath as Dad looked from her to Colin. *Trust me!* She tried to telegraph the plea with her eyes. It must have worked.

Dad folded his napkin and turned to Greg. "All right. I know you guys all gave up your spring vacation to help, and I'm grateful for that. You've got my permission to go." He paused, then said, "If we can get a reasonable amount of work done, and if Anne can spare Wakara and Tia."

Anne met his gaze with a quiet smile. "They are free to go."

"Yippee," Ryan yelled. "We get to go on a raft."

The room went silent. Greg studied his fingernails, and Colin took a long swig from his water glass. Tia started to say something, but Kara flashed her a look, and she shut her mouth. No way would Dad let him go, but Kara wasn't sure how to handle it.

"What about your promise?" Anne spoke quietly and squeezed Ryan's hand.

"What promise?" Ryan scowled.

"You promised to help me catch fish. We must stock the freezer for summer guests."

Ryan perked up. "You mean we're going to Otter Lake?"

Anne nodded. "It is the best place to find trout."

But Ryan wasn't quite convinced. "On horses?"

"We'll work it out, Tiger," Dad broke in, and Kara was glad. They'd have to use the horses to get to the landing where they were going to launch the raft. Dad or Anne would lead the string back, then meet them the next day at the landing closest to the lodge. With Lyman out of commission, they'd really be short of mounts.

The thrill of planning the trip had her mind spinning as she helped Anne clear the table. She had just picked up a stack of dirty plates and started for the kitchen, when her thoughts were shattered by the shrill, sharp barks of an excited dog.

13

"STAY BACK AND BE QUIET," Kara warned Ryan as the little boy tried to squirm out of her hold. She looked at Colin and said, "They're right behind cabin four!"

Dad came up behind them, took Ryan from her, and passed him to Anne. The look on his face stopped the boy in midhowl. "You stay in the house with Anne. No argument!" Dad said. His gaze shifted to Kara, and for one horrible moment she thought he might order her into the house as well. But he didn't. Instead, they stood right where they were, trying to interpret the growls and yips coming from the bear and the dog.

Please don't let any of them get hurt, Kara prayed. In a few minutes the sounds stopped, and the two other rangers came running from the front of the lodge, carrying a folded gurney much like a paramedic would use. Brad came out from behind the cabin and saw Kara and her dad standing there. He waved and called, "Want to see the monster up close?"

Ryan came charging out of the kitchen. Kara reached out to grab him, but Dad scooped him up and carried him toward the waiting rangers.

The bear lay quietly on the ground, and Kara bent to touch the soft, cinnamon-colored fur. "Whoa, he's smaller than I thought!" She stroked the animal's tan snout, then ruffled the white blaze on its chest. "He's like a big teddy bear."

"A 300-pound teddy bear with claws." Brad was grinning at her. "My guess is about three years old. That's young when you consider they can live to be twenty-five. Standing up he'd be about five feet tall, but he still has some growing to do."

Ryan frowned and tugged on Brad's jacket. "You said he was a black bear. How come he's not black?"

Brad bent down to Ryan's level. "You know something about horses, don't you, Ryan?"

Ryan's eyes grew wide, and Kara knew Brad had his full attention. "Sure!"

"Okay," Brad continued. "Is a quarter horse always brown?"

Ryan laughed. "No way. A quarter horse can be lots of colors."

"Right," Brad said, then pointed to the bear. "Black bears are the same. They can be brown or black, cinnamon like this one, or even pure white."

As Ryan's face lit up with understanding, Brad stood and turned to the others. "If anyone else wants to touch him, it has to be quick. We've got to get the radio collar on him and get him to the chopper. If he's not on the ground again before this drug wears off, someone could get hurt."

Tia took two steps backwards, nearly hiding behind Dad, but everyone else petted the bear before the rangers quickly clipped a radio collar around the animal's neck and took him to the chopper. Kara watched as the engine roared to life and the rotor blades lifted the three rangers, the dog,

97

and the bear off the ground. The chopper sped out of sight over the ridge.

While Dad and the guys went to work repainting the water holding tank, Kara and Tia spent the rest of the day scrubbing down cabin five. Heat from last summer's fire had actually scorched the logs on one outside wall, and a thick, white ash covered everything inside. Anne took the bed linens, rugs, and towels into the house to wash.

Ryan was given the job of cleaning the lantern and polishing the small table and dresser they had set outside on the grass. Twice he conned Kara into taking him down to check on Lyman. The horse was restless, but otherwise okay. The wound was still clean and looked like it was healing nicely. Kara gave him another dose of Banamine to help keep him quiet. If he jigged around too much, he might break open the wound. "One more day, boy," she told the fidgety horse, "then we'll turn you into the corral."

The rest of the week went by in a blur of hard work and sore muscles. Kara and Tia talked about Great-grandfather Irish's journal, but no matter how hard they tried to stay awake and read it, they never made it past the first couple of pages. So far all they had learned was how Irish and his partner, a man named Clemens, were making plans to go to California and search for gold.

In an entry dated *June eleventh, year of our Lord 1907*, Irish wrote:

> Clemens is a rough character, uneducated, but he knows the country and insists that gold in the hills east of Sacramento is by no means panned out. He is a trapper besides. He tells me he lived in the wilderness for a year

and not only sustained himself, but came out with enough gold nuggets and animal hides to keep him for two years more. I believe him, though I'm certain he supplements his income by gambling.

It is easy to talk myself into going. After Kathleen's death, there is nothing for me here. I can only think it will be more productive to embark on adventure than to stay here and grieve. Youth and strength are on my side, even if God has chosen to abandon me.

"How awful!" Tia cried.

"Whoa!" Kara agreed. "Who was Kathleen? It sounds like Irish was married before, or at least engaged." But Tia's eyes were already closed. Kara yawned and set the journal aside. She was so tired, the mystery would have to wait.

By Thursday evening most of the heavy work was done, and they all gathered around the fireplace with mugs of cocoa and a huge bowl of popcorn. "We'll get that door on the shed tomorrow morning," Dad said, stretching his feet out toward the hearth. "Everything else is pretty much ready for the normal routine in June."

Kara groaned aloud, and everyone laughed. "The normal routine means cleaning all the rest of the cabins and hauling in enough supplies to feed a small country," she exclaimed.

Ryan scooted closer to Anne. "After tomorrow we'll already have lots of fish."

"We will see," Anne said softly, but her attention was on Greg. "For now, I will go make tea, I think."

99

Greg stumbled to his feet, clutched his stomach, and bolted from the room. Dad jumped up and followed him out the back door.

Kara's stomach churned in sympathy. "Poor Greg. I hope it's not the flu!"

A few minutes later, Dad came back into the room. "Vomiting and low fever. Anybody else sick?" Dad's shoulders drooped, but he studied each of their faces.

"I'm fine." Kara reached over and felt Ryan's forehead. "He's cool." She turned to Tia, who nodded. "Me too."

"I'm okay," Colin said, "but maybe he should sleep in here tonight. I'll bunk on the sofa in the rec room." Dad agreed and went off to get Greg.

Kara and Tia cleaned up the kitchen and set the table for breakfast, while Anne brewed one of her special herb concoctions, set the steaming mug on a tray with a bottle of aspirin, and carried it off toward the bedrooms. When she returned, she reported Greg's stomach had settled a little, and he was asleep.

"What a bummer," Tia moaned as she gathered a handful of silverware to take into the dining room. "With Greg sick, that makes just three of us on the rafting trip." She turned to Kara, "Think Colin will still take us?"

Kara tried to hide her disappointment. "He would, but don't hold your breath; Dad will never go for it."

"Why?" Tia squealed.

"Because Dad's got this thing about me and Colin. He'll never let us go alone."

"What? Wakara, you can't be serious," Tia howled. "I'll be there! Like, you and Colin won't exactly be alone."

Kara's chest felt tight. "Try and tell him that. You're my best friend, Tia. If Dad doesn't trust me, you think he would let the three of us stay alone overnight?"

Anne slid a pan of muffin batter into the refrigerator, then turned to the girls. "It's a father's job to guard his daughter." She put an arm around Kara's shoulders and squeezed. "Better to bow to wisdom and not look temptation in the eye."

Oh, great, Kara thought, *now Anne's on Dad's side.* She turned away. *Coward,* she told herself, *you should have had that talk with Dad a long time ago.*

The lights went out. Dad had turned the generator off. Anne lit the lantern, then set a plate of chocolate cookies on the table, pulled out a chair, and sat down. Kara knew Anne expected her and Tia to stay. All she really wanted was to escape to her room, but that would be rude, and none of this was Anne's fault.

Kara sat down and took a cookie to be polite. Tia grabbed two cookies and downed them with a glass of milk as Anne spoke.

"To the wolf," Anne began, "Creator granted wisdom, unity, and strength. The pack eats, sleeps, plays, and hunts as one. When Alpha Mother gives birth, Alpha Father brings meat to make her rich milk flow. When the pups are weaned, they leave the den to play and learn from others in the pack."

Kara frowned and glanced at Tia. What was Anne getting at? They had learned this stuff in fifth grade. Tia shrugged and grabbed another cookie. If Anne noticed their impatience, it didn't seem to bother her.

"The elders in the pack guard the pups fiercely." Anne continued looking directly at Kara. "They have seen the young carried off by Eagle, or drowned in the raging river. When the pups are mature and have learned their lessons well, they take their place within the order of the pack and join the hunt. A lone wolf cannot survive without the pack.

If even one member dies, the balance is disturbed, and the pack must struggle to find a new order."

Anne stopped talking and sat quietly, obviously waiting for a response.

"I get it," Tia chimed in before Kara could say anything. "The wolf pack is like a family, and kids need to learn from their elders, but I don't understand what that has to do with our rafting trip."

"Or Dad's attitude about me and Colin," Kara shook her head. "I'm almost sixteen, Anne. Dad's always said I was mature for my age. Why can't he trust me now?"

Anne reached over and covered Kara's hand with her own. "Your mother's death has disturbed the balance in your family, Wakara. Your father still struggles to find the order of things. Be patient. Use the wisdom God gave you, and all will be well."

Kara nodded, but she wasn't convinced. What if Dad's struggles went on for a long, long time? *I could be locked in the den until I'm twenty-one!* The silly thought should have made her smile. Instead, she felt a deep sadness. How could she help Dad understand? *Use the wisdom God gave you,* Anne had said, but right now Kara wasn't feeling very wise. Just tired.

Tia yawned hugely and pushed away from the table. "I don't know about you, but I'm going to bed."

Kara stood too. "Thanks, Anne. I guess we'd all better get some sleep. I'll talk to Dad in the morning."

14

IN SPITE OF HOW EXHAUSTED she'd been the night before, Kara awoke before dawn, her mind spinning with ways to approach Dad. Her stomach fluttered uneasily, like it had when she'd watched the video about the Colorado River. *It's like trying to navigate class-five rapids,* she thought, *knowing you have to get through it, but scared you're going to drown.*

She crawled to the end of her bed, careful not to bump into Tia's cot. She pulled on her sweats, then slipped into her fur-lined moccasins. She needed to be alone, and with that bear gone, it would be safe to follow the path to the river. Maybe God would somehow show her what to do.

She slipped out the door, down the hall, and into the recreation room without a sound. At the front door she paused to grab her jacket off the hook, when she heard a cough. Someone was outside on the deck. She cupped her hands around her face and pressed against the window. *Dad!*

He was sitting on the swing at the far end of the deck, staring off into the eastern sky. Kara's heart thumped hard. *Now what?* She could pretend she hadn't seen him and sneak out the back door, but something told her that wouldn't be right.

"Well, God," she whispered, "I guess it's now or never. I could sure use some of that wisdom Anne talked about." She took a deep breath, opened the door, and stepped outside.

"Wakara?" Dad smiled and patted the space next to him on the padded swing. "You're up early. Are you feeling sick?"

Kara shook her head. "No, just couldn't sleep." She shivered. It had rained in the night, and there was still a nip of winter in the damp morning air. "How's Greg?"

"He's pretty sick; he'll need to stay in bed, at least for today." He patted the seat again. When she joined Dad on the swing, he slid an arm around her shoulders and pulled her close. She closed her eyes and relaxed against his shoulder. They hadn't sat like this since she was a little girl. It felt warm and, well, nice. Comforting.

"Your mother and I used to come out here every morning to watch the sun rise over the mountains. It was the best hour of the day for both of us." There was a hint of sadness in Dad's voice, but Kara realized the heavy-hearted sound of grief was gone. Still, she didn't know what to say, so she sat with him and watched as the sky to the east took on a pale pink glow.

Dad shifted and kissed the top of her head. "I owe you an apology, Sugar Bear," he said quietly. "Anne was right. I've been trying to find a new order for our family, and in the process some things have been thrown out of balance. I can't be a mother wolf." He chuckled. "I can't think like that; I don't even know how to try."

Kara sat up straight. "You heard us last night?"

He nodded and went on. "The boys don't even notice, of course, but for a girl there are some things only a mother can handle. I've been an overprotective father, and that hasn't been fair to you."

Kara didn't know what to say. She'd been worried about confronting Dad for being unfair. Now he was apologizing, and she hadn't said a thing.

"So, tell me, Wakara, this, uh," he hesitated, "relationship between you and Colin. How would your mother handle it?"

Kara took a deep breath. "Well," she said slowly, "for one thing, Mom would come to me and find out what the relationship was. She'd want to know how I really feel about Colin."

Dad didn't move a muscle, and Kara could tell he was listening intently. "And what would you tell her?" he asked carefully, almost as if he were holding his breath.

"I don't know, Dad. I like him a lot. He's cute and funny, and I usually have a good time when we do things together. But he makes me crazy with that phony cowboy stuff, and I hate it when he bosses me around." *And I feel nervous and excited when I know we're going to be together.* That was something she would have told Mom, but no way could she say it to Dad. He was still listening, so she decided to talk about something he might understand. "What really makes me crazy is one minute he acts like he wants to be more than friends, and the next minute he treats me like I don't exist. I never know how he really feels about me!"

Dad sighed and gave her shoulders a squeeze before withdrawing his arm and turning to face her. "That's my fault too, I'm afraid. I can see exactly how he feels about you, and I told him to back off."

Kara felt her muscles tighten. She knew he'd said something like that to Colin, but it didn't make it any easier to hear him admit it.

Her anger must have been obvious, because Dad held up his hand. "Give me a minute, please. It's important that you understand." He looked away, ran one hand through his hair, then faced her again. "I like Colin, Wakara, and it would be fine with me if the two of you got together someday, but not yet. I know you don't want to hear this, but you are just too young for that kind of a relationship. And it has nothing to do with trust—you're both good kids, and I know you wouldn't intentionally do anything wrong. It's just better that you maintain a friendship for now, nothing more, okay?"

Better to bow to wisdom and not look temptation in the eye. Those were Anne's words, and they meant the same thing. Kara just nodded. She wanted to know how she and Colin could ever be friends if Dad had told him to stay away from her, but he didn't give her a chance to ask.

"Having said all that," he grinned, "would you still like to go rafting?" She didn't try to hide her surprise, but she still felt like someone had zipped her mouth shut. She managed another nod. "Good. Greg is too sick to be left alone, and I have too many loose ends to tie up. That means Anne's fishing trip with Ryan is off. Why don't you and Tia and Colin make it a day trip and take Ryan along?" She groaned, and his voice softened to an almost pleading tone. "Come on, Sugar Bear. He's had a rough week too. The attack on Lyman really upset him, and now he doesn't get to go fishing either."

Kara knew he was right. "What about Colin? It's his raft."

Dad stood, causing the swing to rock. "I already talked to Colin, and he said it was fine with him."

Kara looked up. Over Dad's shoulder, the eastern sky glimmered with streaks of orange and gold. She sighed. *It's just now sunrise, and I already feel like I've climbed Mount Everest! And,* she thought, *I still have to tell Tia that Ryan is coming along.*

Tia looked sympathetic when Kara told her what Dad had said, but when Kara explained that Ryan had to come along or the trip was off, Tia just shrugged. "Whatever. I guess that's better than not going at all."

Mark arrived in time for breakfast, as usual. "Hey," he said when Colin teased him about it, "a bachelor has to grab

106

a home-cooked meal whenever he can." He winked at Anne. "And this gal's cooking is far better than any four-star restaurant. Maybe I'll just steal her away from you—then you'll appreciate what you've got."

"No need to convince me," Colin said as he reached for the bacon platter. "I know when I'm well off." He grinned at Anne, who blushed and set the basket of blueberry muffins between him and Mark.

Colin turned to Ryan. "Well, Partner, since your fishing buddy is playing nursemaid to Greg, how would you like to help me and these lovely ladies break in my new raft? We've got some scoutin' to do if we're gonna run the Minam River this summer."

Kara wondered how he could sound so cheerful. She knew how much he had been looking forward to running the rapids. The Minam didn't offer much of that.

"Yippee!" Ryan shouted, "I get to go on the raft!" He jumped up from the table. "I'll go get my stuff!" He was out of the room before anyone could call him back.

Mark swallowed a bite of scrambled egg and gestured out the window. "If you're thinking about this part of the river, you'd better think again. After that fire, the spring runoff is carrying a ton of debris. I've flown over it twice this week as far up as the abandoned mill. It'll be months before it cleans itself out. You want a good run, you'll need to go all the way above Finn Rock. It's an easy run back down to the mill. Shouldn't take you more than a day and a half." He took a swallow of orange juice. "Tell you what," he said cheerfully, "after I help Harley with that door, I'll fly you up there. He can come and get you tomorrow afternoon."

The room grew silent. Everyone was looking at Dad. What were the chances he'd agree to that plan? *A big, fat zero!* Kara thought and felt a surge of disappointment. There would be no rafting trip after all.

Mark looked puzzled. "Sorry, Harley, didn't mean to interfere," he said lamely as he reached for his coffee cup.

Tia cleared her throat, and Kara nudged her to be quiet. Her friend sighed and turned her best pleading-puppy face on Dad. Kara almost laughed. That might work with Mr. Sanchez, but no way would it ever work with Dad.

Dad laid his fork down. He had that deer-in-the-head-lights look, and Kara was afraid he might bolt and follow Ryan out of the room. Instead, he threw up his hands and looked at the ceiling. "I may be Alpha Wolf, but I'm not a monster." He glared at Anne. She smiled serenely back at him. Tia put a hand over her mouth to stifle a giggle, and Kara elbowed her again.

"Alpha Wolf?" Poor Mark looked so confused. Kara made the mistake of looking at Tia, and they both burst out laughing.

Dad shook his head. "It's too involved to explain. Let's just say I'll go along with that plan on one condition." Kara held her breath as Dad's gaze settled on Colin, then on her and Tia. "You guys are responsible for Ryan. You stay close to the river at all times, and don't let him out of your sight."

15

IT WAS AFTER TEN O'CLOCK before they were flying over the abandoned mill, about five miles upriver from Eagle Lodge. Mark flew low along the river so they could check out the course. "Looks like it's running a little high," Kara shouted.

Colin nodded. "Yeah, it rained last night." He peered out the window. "Still pretty calm water; we should have an easy run." Kara could hear the disappointment in his voice.

Tia kept her head down. "Ooh, I hate this!" she squealed, and took a firmer grip on Kara's arm. Kara winced and glanced over at Ryan. He didn't much like flying either, but he had taken the other window seat without a fuss and seemed to be enjoying the scenery.

"Wow, look, Kara, there must be a trizillion trees out there!" he yelled.

She laughed. "You're right, Ry, there are, and it's really beautiful right now, isn't it? Everything is so green. Tia, you're really missing out." She jiggled Tia's arm and got a weak, "Ooh," in response.

"Hey, there's a short stretch of white water." Colin's voice held excitement for the first time since they'd taken off.

"That huge bolder in the middle is Finn Rock," Mark said. "Stay to the left and you'll be fine." He leveled out the wings and gained a bit of altitude. The dense forest looked impassable from this distance, but Kara knew there must be deer trails scattered through the area. A few minutes later, she spotted a narrow patch of bare ground directly ahead; just enough room to land a small plane, or so Mark said.

In spite of herself, Kara closed her eyes. She felt a slight bump, then the plane rattled to a stop just a few yards from a thick stand of trees.

Tia let out a moan and scrambled out of the plane after Ryan. Mark and Colin were already unloading the supplies. "Put the raft in over there," Mark suggested, pointing toward a small inlet where the water looked deep and calm. Colin gave him a high five, shouldered the raft, and headed for the riverbank. Kara helped Ryan with his backpack, then handed him his life jacket. "Stay away from the water until you have that on," she shouted as he took off after Colin. She and Tia put on their own packs, gathered up the remaining supplies, and staggered after the boys.

By the time the noise of Mark's plane faded into the distance, the raft was inflated and afloat. Tia held the line, while Kara and Colin loaded their waterproof packs and sleeping bags. Kara helped Ryan buckle his life jacket, then stuffed the rest of the orange vests along the sides within easy reach. She doubted they would need them. From what she had seen from the air, there were no rapids to speak of, and Mark had said this was the only really deep spot on the river.

Kara took the line, while Colin climbed into the bow and fitted the aluminum oars into the oarlocks, which were just a couple of plastic rings, but they would help keep the oars with the boat. Tia and Ryan scrambled into the middle, using the sleeping bags for seats. Kara allowed the raft to float out a little with the current, then hopped in and gave it a push with one of the extra oars. She and Colin rowed,

110

smoothly matching each other's strokes, until they were moving along at a pretty good pace.

"Hey, you better slow down so I can catch some fish." Ryan dug through his pack and came up with his collapsible fishing pole, hooks, and a small jar of salmon eggs.

"Yuck!" Tia wrinkled her nose. "I hope you can bait the hook yourself, Small Fry, because I'm not touching those slimy things."

Kara sighed, pulled her oars out of the water, and stored them along the sides of the raft. "Here, Ry, I'll help you get the hook on, then you're on your own." *And if you believe that, Dorothy, you'd better go back to Kansas.* From the smirk on Colin's face, she knew he was thinking the same thing.

After an hour of helping Ryan untangle his line, baiting his hook, and rescuing the oar he managed to knock overboard, Kara sank back into the boat with a groan. "I thought this was supposed to be relaxing!"

Colin took pity on her. "I don't know about you guys, but I could use some lunch. Why don't you reel in, Partner, and break out some of those cheese crackers we brought along?"

"I guess," Ryan grumbled. "There's no fish in this stupid river anyway."

Kara rolled her eyes, but didn't have the strength to lecture him. She yawned and settled back into the curve of the raft. The sky was clear, with a just few puffs of white cloud. A warm breeze teased a strand of hair across her cheek, and the raft rocked gently on the calm water.

"Wakara?"

Kara felt a hand on her shoulder and opened her eyes. The raft was no longer moving, and when she took Colin's offered hand and pulled herself up, she saw they were grounded in shallow water along a sandy shore.

Colin grinned. "Come on, Sleeping Beauty, you may be small, but we can't beach this thing with you still in it."

"Whoa, sorry. I must have dozed off."

"I guess!" Tia reached past her for one of the sleeping bags. "You were cutting Zs for over two hours!"

Kara felt her face burn. Colin let go of her arm, gathered up a couple of backpacks, and moved off to where Ryan was gathering rocks. Kara grabbed the back of Tia's shirt. When her friend turned around, Kara whispered, "I didn't really snore, did I?"

Tia laughed. "No. It's just an expression. Sorry. But you were really out of it."

Impulsively, Kara gave her a hug. "I guess I didn't sleep very well last night." Really, she hadn't slept much at all. Tia on the other hand had snored loudly enough to rouse a hibernating bear.

Colin came back, and the three of them pulled the raft onto the sand. "This is a great place to spend the night," he said when they had the raft secure. "That big log over there makes a perfect windbreak for the fire. I can even bed down in front of it, and the rest of you can lay out your bags in that circle of trees."

Tia looked around. "Fine by me, as long as we eat pretty soon. I'm starved!"

Kara frowned. "There's still a lot of daylight left. If we stop now, will we make it on time tomorrow?"

"Hey, Kara," Ryan hollered. "Come see what I found. Flat rocks, and they're the perfect size." He let one fly, and Kara jumped back as it sailed between her and Colin, then landed with a plop in the water.

"Ryan Sheridan!" But he was already headed the other direction.

"This place is cool; I'm gonna explore!" he called back over his shoulder.

"I'll get him." Tia sprinted across the clearing. "Come back here, you little squirt. You have to stay with us."

"I do not!" Ryan yelled. "And don't call me Squirt!"

Kara groaned and plopped down on a log. Colin laughed. "You really want to get back into the boat?" She shook her head. He held out her jacket and lifted a small mess kit out of the raft. "The river runs downhill from here. We should make landing in plenty of time to meet your dad."

The wind off the water sent goose bumps up Kara's arms. She pulled on her heavy jacket, snagged the last sleeping bag, and hurried over to help set up camp. When they were done, Colin gathered up the fishing gear and took Ryan upriver. Kara flashed him a look of gratitude, then turned to Tia. "Now what?"

Tia grinned. "Now," she said, "we explore!"

Away from the water, the temperature was actually mild. Mosquitoes were already hatching in muddy pools where the rainwater had not yet dried up, and black flies buzzed around their ears. They swatted the pests and kept walking, following a slim trail that ran parallel to the river. Kara pointed out deer scat and the tracks of a raccoon.

"I hope those are the only animals around."

Tia sounded nervous, so Kara just said, "Don't worry about it," trying to sound calm. She decided not to point out the larger tracks she'd seen crossing the trail. She didn't stop to examine them, either. Not that she was afraid. If they kept the fire going tonight, most animals would stay away.

You think that little fire is going to keep a bear away? She stepped over a fallen log. *But it should,* she argued with herself. That bear at Eagle Lodge had been a rogue, and the one back in Lariat had probably been scared to death when she and Lily came galloping across the meadow toward her cub. *Black bears are by nature shy,* she told herself, *and a group of four humans should be enough to deter one bear.*

She and Tia had just made it back to camp when Colin and Ryan came into the clearing. "Good timing, ladies." Colin grinned and held up a string of fish. "Dinner is served!"

"Trout!" Ryan shouted, as if they weren't standing right there. "I caught the big one; look, he's a whopper!"

Colin winked at Kara and steered Ryan toward the river. "Come on, Partner, we're not done yet. What you catch, you clean."

Kara started a fire, while Tia dug through the packs. "Three packages of stroganoff mix. That should be enough." Tia glanced at the shoreline, where Colin was scouring his fishing knife with sand. "You can have my share of the trout," she whispered.

Kara laughed. "Don't worry, the guys won't care if you don't eat any. It'll be that much more for them."

Colin coated the fish in cornmeal, unfolded a small aluminum fry pan, and cooked them one at a time in the butter Anne had sent along. When everyone had eaten, there was nothing left but bones and one spoonful of noodles in the bottom of the pan. Kara scraped the garbage into a plastic bag. "That was great, Ry. Thanks for catching dinner."

Ryan beamed. "I'll get some more tomorrow."

Kara started to tell him they wouldn't have time to fish tomorrow. They had to stay on the water if they were going to make it back on time, but she decided not to stir up an argument. They were having too much fun. She and Tia cleaned up the pans and dishes, while Colin rifled through his bag and produced a flattened bag of white goo. "Marshmallows." He grinned. "I guess they got kind of squashed."

"So?" Ryan piped up. "They still taste good."

Colin nodded. "You know, Partner, I think you're right." He broke off a sticky, white blob, threaded it onto a green twig, and handed it to Ryan.

114

When they'd all eaten their fill of the gooey dessert, Ryan wiped his hands on his jeans and said, "Hey, let's tell ghost stories! I bet Colin knows some good ones."

Kara flashed Colin a warning glare. She breathed a sigh of relief when he said with a drawl, "Sorry, Partner, but I know for a fact that there are no ghosts in these woods." He paused and rubbed his chin, playing the part of storyteller to the hilt. "Although I do believe they've seen a Sasquatch in the area."

Tia groaned, and Kara shook her head. "Colin," she warned, but he refused to look at her. He had Ryan's attention, though.

"What's a Sasquatch?"

"You know," Colin's voice dropped to an ominous whisper, "Big Foot."

"Big Foot!" Ryan's eyes were as big as dinner plates. "You mean that hairy monster that looks like a bear-man and has footprints bigger than a grizzly?"

Colin nodded soberly, and Kara said, "Come on, Ry, Colin's only kidding you. They haven't even proven Big Foot exists. And even if he does," she glared at Colin, "he's not wandering around in this valley."

"He does too exist!" said Ryan. "I saw it on TV. They have pictures and everything." Then his shoulders drooped, and he patted Colin's arm. "It's okay, Colin, I just remembered. The TV guy said Big Foot is really shy. He'd never hurt anyone." He yawned and leaned his head against Kara's arm. "I think I'm sorta sleepy."

Tia stood and stretched. "Well, Wakara may have had a nap, but I didn't, so if you two don't mind, I'm going to crash." Ryan was already asleep. Colin helped Tia spread the space blankets in the curve of trees on the other side of the fire, then he rolled out the sleeping bags on top of them. He helped Kara bundle Ryan into one bag, then spread out his own bedroll next to the fallen log and sat back down by the fire.

"Way to go, Colin," Kara said. "It's a good thing he wasn't scared, or you would have been the one up with him all night."

He grinned. "He's a smart kid, he'll be fine." He patted the spot next to him. "Come sit awhile."

He must have seen her hesitate, because his grin faded and he lowered his voice. "It's okay, Wakara. I had a long talk with your Dad. He wouldn't have let us come if he weren't convinced I would treat you with respect. I was pretty sure you already knew that."

Relieved, Kara sat down next to him. "I do know that," she said quietly, then stared into the fire, hoping Colin couldn't hear the thudding of her heart. "About Dad." She made herself look up at Colin. "I'm sorry you had to go through all that. He's just being . . ." She couldn't quite form the right words.

"An Alpha Wolf?" Colin supplied them for her, and they both laughed.

Kara took a deep breath and leaned back against the log. "I really love being in the woods. It makes me feel so content and peaceful, and, well, free!"

Colin shifted around until he was facing her. "What do you want, Wakara?" he asked. "Out of life, I mean."

She sighed, then began to tell him all about her plans to be a vet and her desire to live in a small town, close to farms and ranches, so she could specialize in large animals like horses and cattle.

Colin said little, just encouraged her with nods and murmurs of approval. When she realized she had been babbling for over half an hour, she stopped and tossed another log onto the fire. "All right, your turn." She grinned up at him.

He smiled back at her and plopped his hat onto her head. "You look better in my hat than I do."

Colin's hair was flattened against his scalp, except for a swirl of hair standing straight up from the cowlick on the crown of his head. Kara giggled. "You look like Alfalfa in the *Our Gang* shows." She shook off the hat, coiled her long, black braid on top of her head, then put the hat back on. "But that's not going to get you out of this, Colin Jones."

He flashed her an innocent look. "Out of what?"

She took off his hat and held it over the fire. "I told you my dreams, now it's your turn!" She dangled the hat by one finger, but kept her thumb on the brim for balance in case he made a grab for it.

"Okay, okay, give it back, please? See, I'm not too proud to beg." She jiggled the hat again. "All right," he groaned, "you win! I want to be a rancher with a wife and six kids and breed horses—Friesians, to be exact—and I want to grow old and sit on the porch in a rocking chair with my feet propped on the railing and my wife by my side." He grinned and reached for his hat. "How's that for old-fashioned values?"

She let go of the hat, and he snatched it just before it hit the fire. "You don't believe me?"

He sounded so wounded that Kara finally relented. "Friesians? Are you serious?" Friesians were gorgeous horses, bred mostly for show. And they were huge—not to mention expensive.

He nodded. "Friesians. I've almost got enough cash saved for the first mare. Another two years and I should have the down payment on that twenty-acre parcel over by the Carlson's."

Where do the wife and kids come in? she wanted to ask. Instead she said, "That's neat, Colin, it really is." She scrambled to her feet, hoping he would think the flush on her face was from the blazing campfire. "I'd better get to bed." She tried to sound casual, but her voice squeaked when she said, "Good night."

Away from the fire the air was cold, but inside she felt like she was running a fever. She scooted down into her sleeping bag, slipped off her jacket and shoes, and stuffed them into the bottom of the bag, where they would stay warm and dry until morning. She tried to think about something else, but images of herself and Colin clicked like snapshots through her mind: kneeling beside a newborn foal—riding double on a huge Friesian stallion—rocking together on a wide front porch. The last image almost made her laugh out loud. She pulled the edge of her sleeping bag over her head, leaving just her nose sticking out. It was nice to share your dreams with someone you cared for, and right now, she realized, she cared for Colin Jones a lot.

16

KARA AWOKE TO BRIGHT SUN in an ice blue sky. She reached down into the sleeping bag for her jacket and shoes, shook Tia and Ryan awake, then joined Colin by the fire, holding her hands over the dancing flames. Colin already had the coffee perking and a pan of water warming on the rocks. "No use roughing it any more than we have to." He grinned and motioned to the water. "It should be warm enough. Ladies first."

"Thanks!" She took the pan, shouldered her pack, and hustled a sleepy Tia ahead of her into the woods. Ten minutes later, she set the pan filled with clean river water over the fire. When it was warm enough, Colin took Ryan with him, while Kara boiled fresh water from one of the canteens in a smaller aluminum pan, then added instant oatmeal.

"Amazing how everything tastes better when you're camping." Tia spooned up the last of her oatmeal. "I don't even like this stuff at home."

Kara laughed. "Mom always said the fresh air makes you hungry. She loved to camp. We used to go up into the Three Sisters Wilderness for two weeks at a time in the summer, remember, Ryan?" He nodded, and she went on, lost in the memory. "We had this old canvas army tent—big enough

119

for an army, too. And cold!" She shivered. "It was like sleeping in a cave."

Colin grinned. "Give me a good sleeping bag and a bed of pine boughs any day!" He squeezed her shoulder and said to Ryan, "Come on, Partner, let's get your stuff together. If we're going to get that raft back on the water anytime soon, we have to break camp now."

By the time Kara tugged Ryan's life vest over his jacket, the sun had reached ten o'clock high. "What have you got in there?" she asked as she struggled to fit the vest around Ryan's bulging pockets.

"Stuff!" He glared at her and clutched both jacket pockets as if to keep her from looking in. Not that it mattered. They were zipped closed.

Kara frowned. "Well, can't you put some of it in your backpack? This is so bulky, I can hardly get it fastened."

He shook his head. "No! It's my survival kit. I might need it."

Kara sighed and finally clicked the plastic buckle shut. "Fine with me, but don't complain if this is too tight. Going without it isn't an option."

"Let's go," Colin called, and everyone scrambled to the same seats they'd had the day before. Tia stayed quiet, and Kara could tell her friend was still sleepy. Ryan chattered and pointed out every bird and chipmunk in sight. Once they saw a deer drinking at the water's edge. It stared at them as they floated past, then lowered its head to drink again.

"Look, Kara, he's friendly." Ryan watched until the deer was out of sight.

Kara smiled. "He doesn't see many people back in here, Ry. He hasn't learned to be afraid."

She paddled with Colin until the main current picked up, carrying them smoothly downstream.

They'd been on the river for about half an hour when Kara felt the raft shift from a smooth glide to a bumpy rocking motion. Then she heard the sound of rushing water. "Shh, listen." The sound reminded her of Tunnel Falls. She shivered as she always did when she remembered how Ryan nearly plunged over the edge the day they escaped from the fire.

Everyone in the boat stopped talking, and then Colin grinned. "White water!"

Kara laughed at the gleam in his eyes. "It's that stretch by Finn Rock. We saw it from the air," she reminded him. "Mark said it wasn't bad if we stay to the left."

Colin nodded. "Nothing on this river is above a class three. Still, I should row from the back so I can see where we're going. Help me turn the raft, Wakara." Then he grinned again. "Sorry, hope you don't mind getting wet."

She gave him what she hoped was the stern warning look her mother had always used on Greg.

"From what I saw, there's no reason for anyone to get wet, Colin Jones, as long as you behave!"

"Who, me?" He looked so wounded that for a second she felt badly for doubting him. Then, just before the raft swung around, she caught the spark of mischief in his eyes.

"Colin! What are you going to do?" She had to practically shout over the sound of rushing water as the boat picked up speed.

"Trust me, Wakara," he shouted back. "I know what I'm doing."

Kara knew she had to turn around and face the front. She needed to have her oars ready to push them away from the rocks. But first she had to be sure Ryan and Tia knew what to do. "Ryan," she yelled, "put your backpack down and sit in the bottom of the boat. Tia, anchor your knee under the rim and hang on to him, please!"

"What's the big deal? I thought this was a no-brainer." The look on Tia's face reminded Kara of a trapped rabbit, but she felt a rush of relief as both her friend and Ryan pushed aside their makeshift seats and scrambled to the bottom of the raft.

"Look to the right, Wakara," Colin hollered as she turned around to face the rapids. "Short and sweet. Let's go for it!" She started to scream, "Colin, no!" But it was already too late.

The front end of the raft dipped, then rose on the first wave. Kara paddled furiously, then realized that with her short arms the oar didn't quite reach the water. Before she could even blink, the nose of the raft plunged into a trough, and the current spun them sideways. The thunk of the oar hitting rock sent vibrations up her arm. They spun again, nose first, into a wall of white water. Colin was screaming something, but she couldn't make out the words over the roar of the waves. She saw the boulder coming at them for the second time and punched at it with the oar. The raft bounced back into the swirling current.

Whirlpool! A rush of fear made her body shudder as the raft spun around for the third time. Kara knew if they didn't get out of the spinning water soon, they'd be sucked under and drown. Again, the boulder loomed in front of her. This time she waited until the last minute, then shifted forward, shoved both oars against the rock, and pushed with all of her might.

The force knocked her backwards. One oar snapped, and Kara felt the plastic paddle whiz by her ear. Tia screamed, and Kara scrambled to her knees. For one sickening moment they hung suspended at the top of a wave, then, like a rock from a giant slingshot, the raft shot backwards out of the swirling water.

"My backpack!" Ryan's yell hit her like a stomach punch, and she watched in horror as the boy threw himself onto the side of the boat, arms stretched toward the backpack floating just out of reach. "Ryan, no!" she screamed. She lunged after him just as the current caught the raft and propelled them downstream.

Everything seemed to happen in slow motion after that. Her body collided with Colin's as they both made a grab for Ryan's legs. Then the raft plunged once more into a short patch of white water, knocking her flat on her back. Again, she pushed to her knees. Just as the raft shot around a bend in the river, she caught a glimpse of orange bobbing in the water close to shore.

The current slowed, and the roar of waves was replaced by the slap of Colin's oars as he propelled them toward an inlet of calm water that lapped against an eroded bank. A sudden jolt and the raft stopped dead about five feet from shore.

"A tree! We're hung up on a tree!" Kara heard the sob in Colin's voice. Her brain registered the fear and frustration she saw on his face. She should tell him not to panic. Help him get the raft untangled. Get them all safely on shore. But she couldn't move. *Ryan.* Her little brother was no longer in the boat. She had to find him, but when she tried to move, her arms wouldn't cooperate. Her legs felt numb, and she felt as if her mind had been sucked into another whirlpool.

"Wakara! Tia's bleeding. She's unconscious. Come on, snap out of it, you've got to help me!"

Someone was shaking her. As she looked up into Colin's fear-twisted face, all she felt was a cold, steady anger. "Get your hands off me, Colin Jones." She heard her own voice, like ice cracking in a drinking glass. Her mouth felt dry and tasted like wood shavings from Lily's stall. Her hands felt clammy as she raised them to his chest and shoved him away.

Colin lost his balance and fell into Tia. Kara cringed as the girl howled like a banshee, then sat up holding her head. "Ooh. What happened? I feel like someone hit me with a brick."

"Let me look." Colin peeled Tia's hands away, and Kara could see a thin, red line running from the girl's hairline to the bridge of her nose. The cut was still seeping blood, and Kara moved forward for a closer look. "It's not deep." She grabbed her backpack, dug out the first aid kit, and thrust it at Colin. "Take care of her. I've got to get Ryan!"

As she pushed to her feet, the raft rocked violently, causing Tia to squeal, but it didn't turn over or float free. It took Kara only a moment to see they were caught in a tangle of twisted branches from a fallen tree. She scanned the area for another way out. She could easily swim the five feet or so to shore, but the riverbank was high and so eroded there were no handholds to help her climb.

Fear, sharp as an eagle's beak, ripped through her as she realized they were trapped. But the vision of a bright orange life jacket bobbing in the river sent her up onto the edge of the raft. How long had Ryan been in the water? Had the current washed him into shore, or onto the rocks? Whatever, she had to get to him, and fast!

17

KARA CLAWED THROUGH THE tangled branches until her hands closed around the slim trunk of the fallen tree. She shook it hard, then, when it didn't break away from the bank, she shook it harder. Still, it held. She crouched, then willed her legs to act like springs as she hurtled herself into the center of the tree. Heart pounding, she straddled the trunk for a few seconds to catch her breath. Colin was yelling something about being careful, but she wasn't interested in anything he had to say. Ryan was in trouble, and they'd already wasted enough time.

She pulled herself along the slender trunk, ignoring the sting of pain as twigs scraped her face and poked into her hands. Seconds later she reached the spot where the tree clung to the bank by a tangle of exposed roots. She grabbed a handful of the slippery wood and pushed with her feet, launching herself upward. She landed hard on her belly, her fingers digging into solid ground. A few more inches and her knees gained hold. She jumped to her feet and sprinted downriver, pushing through the brush until she found a slim trail close to the water's edge.

Panting from the exertion, she forced herself to slow down and scan the water as she moved along. Ryan couldn't have floated by them. That bright orange life jacket would be hard to miss. She studied the river and the opposite shore, peering under the ledges of the higher banks, scanning the underbrush at the water's edge. The roar of white water once again filled her ears. The ground angled slightly uphill as she rounded a curve and spotted the huge boulder with the patch of churning water just a few feet below. It looked almost harmless from here. In fact, the rapids on the left side of Finn Rock resembled little more than a long, rippled slide. Like a ride at a water park.

At first glance, the right side looked almost as unthreatening. Then, as Kara studied the current, she recognized with a sickening jab of fear the whirling spiral of water that could suck even a bigger raft than Colin's down a spinning funnel to certain death.

She shuddered, then forced herself to study the area where she'd last seen Ryan. He'd gone out of the boat a few feet downriver from the rapids. *It's not likely he would have been sucked back into the whirlpool from there.* The thought made her feel a little better. He'd fallen toward this side, away from the current that had carried the raft straight and fast down the middle of the river. The last she'd seen of him was the life vest bobbing toward shore.

There! Kara's breath caught as she spied a patch of orange at the water's edge just a few feet downriver from where she was standing. Arms out, she balanced herself and slid on her heels down the slight embankment. She sprinted over slippery stones, nearly falling into the ankle-deep water. In seconds she was in a small cove, where shallow waves lapped at a patch of mud-colored sand. She skidded to a stop and sank to her knees beside Ryan's empty, bright orange vest.

He made it to shore! Joy flooded through her, then quickly ebbed as she realized there was no sign of her brother in the cove. She looked around. No footprints either. "Ry?"

126

She'd meant to yell, but her voice came out a whisper. She stood, cupped her hands around her mouth, and screamed, "Ryan! Where are you?"

She heard a rustling in the bushes and spun around as a blue jay squawked and flew into the upper branches of a skinny pine. "Ry!" She cupped her hands and tried again.

"Wakara?"

At the sound of her name, she jumped and turned. "Colin!"

His face was the color of ashes. "Wakara, I'm sorry. I came to help."

She steeled herself against his apology and tore her gaze from his pleading eyes. "Then help." Once again Kara felt like an ice queen, but she didn't care. It was Colin's fault they were in this mess. If he'd paid attention to Mark's warning and stayed on the left side of the rocks, they'd be almost home by now, and her little brother would be safe.

She spun around and led the way back to the cove. "Here's his vest. It's unbuckled. He has to be around here somewhere, but I can't find any tracks."

"Maybe the vest came off upriver and floated here on its own."

Kara felt frozen in place. "What are you saying? That the vest came off and my brother is still in the river?" The fury in her voice startled them both. Colin reached out, then drew back away from her.

"I'm sorry, Wakara, but we have to look at that possibility."

Kara forced herself to think. The vest had been hard to buckle over Ryan's jacket. The impact with the water could have caused it to come undone. But she couldn't face that yet. "It's also possible he made it to shore, got rid of the vest, and wandered off somewhere." She gestured toward the woods. "He was probably stunned. In fact, he could be close—just not able to hear us call."

Colin nodded. "Tia's still a little woozy. The paddle from one of your oars is missing. It must have broken off and hit her in the head. The bleeding is stopped, and I wrapped her in one of the sleeping bags, so she should be okay for a while." He took a deep breath. "We'll look for half an hour, then go for help."

Kara heard him, but was too busy scanning the area to really listen. "I know he's on this side of the river. I'm going this way as far as I can along the bank." She gestured toward the woods again. "You go up there. Crisscross the area inland, back toward the raft. We didn't bring the walkie-talkies, so shout if you find him. Sound should travel well in here."

Colin nodded and bent to pick up the vest.

"Leave it!" Kara snapped. "It will make it easier to find this spot."

Without waiting for a reply, she turned and jogged along the shoreline, calling Ryan's name. When she was forced to higher ground, she continued along as close to the bank as she could, searching the underbrush and even looking up into the lower limbs of trees her brother might have climbed. The terrain became steeper, and many times she was forced to climb over huge boulders, then scramble down the other sides.

Half an hour later, her heart was pounding in her ears and her legs felt like jelly, but there was still no sign of Ry. Fear hit her like a fist in the belly when she realized the seven year old could never have come this far. *Colin might be right. Ryan could still be in the river.* But if he was still in the river, that meant he had drowned. She dropped to her knees on the ground. Her mind felt numb. She couldn't believe that, not when there was still a chance.

God has not given you a spirit of fear. Anne's voice filtered into her thoughts, but Kara mentally shoved the half-remembered verse to the back of her mind. She didn't know where God fit into this, she only knew she was too numb to pray and too scared to do anything but keep on looking for her brother.

"Wakara!" Her name echoed through the forest like a shotgun blast.

"Colin?" He had promised to yell. That must mean he'd found Ry! She jumped to her feet and ran toward the voice. "Wakara!" There it came again. She raced inland, dodging trees and brush. Still, the going up here was easier, and she forced herself on, following Colin's voice, until she came to a clearing not far from where they had left the raft.

Doubled over and fighting for air, she nearly tumbled into Colin's arms. "Where is he?" she gasped. She looked around as Colin held her steady.

"Take it easy." He pulled her close and she gave in, laying her head against his chest until she caught her breath. When she recovered enough to stand on her own, she realized that, except for her and Colin, the clearing was empty.

"Where is he?" she asked again.

Colin shook his head. "I couldn't find him, Wakara. I covered the area between here and the rapids twice, but there's no sign. Think about it," he said when she pushed him away. "Look around you. It's like trying to find a needle in a haystack."

Kara felt stunned, and the fight went out of her like air from a balloon. Colin took her arm and led her out of the clearing. The sound of water rushing over rock was soothing. If she could just lie down and close her eyes, the river would lull her to sleep.

The raft was tied up a few yards downstream from the fallen tree, and Kara realized Colin must have somehow worked it free. As they got closer, she spied Tia huddled under a sleeping bag in the bottom of the boat. Her friend's eyes were red from crying, and the whole top of her face was swollen clear to the hairline.

"Did you find him?" Tia's voice was slurred, and Kara realized Colin must have given her a dose of the painkiller they kept in the first aid kit for emergencies.

Colin shook his head. "No. And there's no way we will. Not on our own." He tightened his grip on Kara's arm. "In you go, Princess. We've done what we can—now we go for help."

18

KARA FELT LIKE SHE'D JUST hiked the Grand Canyon from one end to the other. Her feet throbbed, and her knees were trembling from fatigue. *We do need help,* she silently agreed with Colin.

The woods were too big, the area along the river too dense for them to cover every foot of it on their own.

Colin stepped into the raft, turned around, and held out his hand. "Come on, Wakara. Tia needs a doctor, and we can radio for divers as soon as we get back to the lodge."

"Divers?" Kara felt her limbs go cold. Her entire body was shaking, but not from the temperature. If Colin thought she was going to give up that easily, it was obvious he didn't know her at all. She took his hand and stepped into the boat. When he was seated at the bow, oars in hand, she grabbed her backpack with the sleeping bag strapped to the frame and tossed it onshore, then scooped up the first aid kit and jumped out of the raft.

"Wakara! Don't be an idiot. Get back in the boat!" Colin's voice radiated fear and frustration. She ignored him until she was a safe distance from the raft. Then she said evenly, "Ryan had a life jacket, and he's had survival training. He is not dead, Colin Jones, and I'm not leaving until I find him!"

"Wakara, please." He looked so defeated, Kara almost relented, but she steeled herself against his pleading eyes.

"She won't leave," Tia's voice broke on a sob. "I'm sorry, Wakara. I'd stay and help if I could, but I really feel sick."

Concern for her friend softened Kara's tone, but not her resolve. "Get going." She stared past Colin's shoulder so she wouldn't have to look at his tear-stained face. "Send in Search-and-Rescue as fast as they can get here. I'll be around." Then she scooped up her pack and sprinted into the woods.

When she was out of sight, she stopped to listen. The sound of Tia's sobs grew fainter, and Kara knew Colin had taken off. Dad was supposed to meet them at the old mill by six o'clock. That was five hours from now. By then it would be almost dark.

Kara strapped on her pack and began to walk again, following a zigzag course upstream along the river. When she came to the spots where boulders blocked her way, she went around, calling loudly as she walked. Had it been only three short hours since she had buckled Ryan into his life jacket and helped him into the boat?

Ryan can't be dead. God wouldn't let that happen.

But Mom died.

God saved us from the fire. He'll save us now.

Why should He? You haven't even prayed. The thought stopped her cold. She hadn't prayed, she realized, not once. She'd been too intent on finding Ryan.

"There are no problems too big for God, but a stubborn heart can muffle His voice." Where had she heard that before? Anne, of course. Anne had the answer to everything. *Well, Anne isn't here, and I don't have time to pray right now!*

She pushed her thoughts aside and struggled through the brush next to the water's edge, searching the riverbanks in and out of the water. She bent down and peered under ledges where a body might lodge. She would never admit Ry was dead, but he could be unconscious and hung up on a tree branch or something, just like the raft had been. She swatted at the huge black flies that buzzed around her ears and face, and brushed away mosquitoes that attacked every time she stopped to call Ryan's name. When she came to the spot where she'd found Ryan's life vest, she worked her way inland and followed a deer trail upstream. She watched the ground carefully, looking for tracks. She spotted deer droppings and antler rubs on trees. Prints of small animals told her this trail was well used, but there were no human footprints to be seen.

When her legs threatened to dump her to the ground, Kara plopped down on a stump and listened to the sounds of the forest. Blue jays squabbled over a patch of early berries, and squirrels scampered from tree to tree as if the intertwining branches were freeways they traveled to and from their homes. Any other time the thought would have made her smile. Now she was too tired to feel much of anything. The vague sickness in her stomach turned to rumbling, and she knew she needed to eat if she wanted strength to continue the search.

She dug through her pack and found a squashed package of raisins, two fruit rolls, some trail mix, and three strips of beef jerky. She settled for the trail mix and a box of juice, then looked at her watch. It was only four o'clock. Colin and Tia still had at least an hour on the river and another hour before they met up with Dad. They'd never get Search-and-Rescue in here before dark.

A new rush of tears warmed her cheeks. *That means it's up to me.* She closed her eyes and tried to think. Where should she search? *Farther inland?* She shook her head. *No.*

Ryan would stay near the river. Back downstream, past where they'd grounded the raft?

"Where is he, God? You've got to help me. Show me where to look!" It wasn't really a prayer, more like an angry demand. And that's exactly how she felt: angry, desperate, and deserted by God. And Colin's betrayal hurt almost as badly as Ryan being lost. He had made a choice to run the wilder rapids. He had deliberately put them all in danger. She would never be able to forgive him for that.

Kara stood and strapped her backpack over her jacket. The afternoon sun didn't penetrate into the forest. It would be cold tonight. She was dry, but Ryan had been in the river. If he was unconscious and unable to get warm, he could freeze to death. *Some choice,* she thought bitterly, *freeze or drown.* She hurried down the deer trail, not stopping to call or even catch her breath until she reached the clearing where she'd met Colin a few hours earlier. There'd been no sign of Ryan between here and the rapids. Was it possible he'd been carried past them downstream? The current had been pretty fast, but the river wasn't deep. Surely they would have him. Besides, his life jacket was on shore a long ways back. Even if it had come off in the water, it made sense to think Ryan would have been washed ashore at about the same place. *And what about his backpack!* she reasoned. There'd been no sign of it, either. Ryan must have caught it and carried it with him away from the river. Maybe the water level had risen for some reason and washed his footprints away.

And maybe pigs can fly. She shook her head. *Get over it, Wako. All this maybe stuff won't find him.* She had to keep on looking.

When she reached the tree where they had been hung up in the raft, she shed her pack and shimmied out onto the trunk. The branches dipped perilously close to the water, but held her weight. For once, she was glad to be small. The tree limbs carried her almost to the middle of the river. She sat up, and when she was balanced, searched the river and its high, brush-choked banks. It was a long, straight stretch of water, but it was like sitting in the end zone of a football field. Things were pretty clear for the first fifty yards, but after that details were blurred. As far as she could tell though, there was no sign of a backpack, or a little boy wearing blue jeans and a dark green jacket.

He made it to shore. He's disoriented. He's holed up somewhere and can't hear me call. Her mind spun with possibilities as she resumed the search, this time walking a zigzag course downstream, inland from the river. It was nearly dark when she heard the sound of the chopper blades.

Kara felt a surge of hope. Colin and Tia had sent help! She dropped her pack and unzipped the outside pocket, searching wildly for the waterproof matches she always kept there. She had to light a fire or the chopper would never see her in this light. She ran toward the sound of the churning engine, then froze. A feeling of sharp despair nearly brought her to her knees. *So what if they find me? Ryan's the one who needs rescuing.* It was almost dark. If she got into that chopper, they would take her back to Eagle Lodge and suspend the search for Ryan until morning.

She hurried back to where she'd left her pack and practically dove into a cluster of juniper and wild rhododendron bushes. A squirrel scolded her from the nearest tree, and a pair of crows took flight, setting up enough ruckus to stampede a herd of cattle. Thankfully, the chopper crew wasn't looking for crows.

Kara made herself as small as possible and held her breath as the helicopter passed overhead. It flew slowly, stopping every few yards to hover. She knew they were trying to cover every foot of ground between here and the rapids. She hoped they wouldn't stop until they had. *Please, please don't let them see me; they have to keep searching, they have to.*

"I will never leave you, or forsake you."

That Bible verse was not the answer she'd expected from her desperate prayer. *"It's not me I'm scared for,"* she wanted to shout, *"it's Ryan. I don't want anything for myself, God. Please just let us find him!"*

She huddled in her hiding place until the sky grew dark. The helicopter made one more pass with its searchlight blazing only inches from her hunched over form. She squeezed her eyes shut and listened as the engine noise faded into the night. She knew they would not be back until morning.

19

WHEN SHE WAS SURE THE helicopter wasn't coming back, Kara dug a flashlight out of her pack and started inland, looking for a grove of trees where she might find wood to build a tepee and start a fire. She'd gone only a couple hundred yards when she tripped. She caught hold of a tree to keep from falling, then trained the flashlight on the ground to where a wooden stake held down a piece of rope. She followed the rope with her light and gasped when she found an old, square-frame shelter covered with a green canvas tarp, almost identical to the one Dad had used with their old army tent.

Kara could hardly believe it! She peered cautiously inside. The shelter was empty, and from the looks of things, no human had occupied it for awhile. She scooped out old pine branches littered with animal droppings and small bones. She studied the debris carefully, then decided none of it was fresh enough to worry about. When the floor of the small shelter was clean, she cut some fresh pine boughs, laid them down, and covered them with a space blanket. She was so tired, it took every ounce of energy she had just to crawl inside, roll into her sleeping bag, and close her eyes.

When she awoke, the thick darkness had given way to a million stars winking like diamonds in an ink blue sky. The world outside her sleeping bag was sharp with cold, and her face and nose felt numb. She rubbed some feeling into her cheeks, then looked at her watch. The luminous dial told her it was close to 11:00 P.M. Her stomach churned, reminding her that it had been hours since her last meal.

Keeping as much of her body as possible in the sleeping bag, she rifled through her pack and found the raisins, a piece of jerky, and her canteen of water. She wanted more than anything to look for Ryan, but she knew better than to try. The woods were no place to roam in the dark. She could only hope and pray that he was holed up like she was, safe and warm.

She chewed the dry meat, enjoying the salty, smoky flavor. If Ryan had managed to grab his backpack, he wouldn't go hungry either. The packs were waterproof, and he had a change of clothes, not to mention extra socks and a sweatshirt. *He'll be fine.* She tried to convince herself of that, but the tears came anyway, and she knew there was a good chance he wasn't fine. A good chance he wasn't even alive.

Don't think like that, Wako, it doesn't help.

"Cast all your anxiety on Him, for He cares for you."

First Peter 5:7. They had memorized that verse at youth group a few weeks ago, and Mr. Andrews had given the illustration of anxiety or worries being like a heavy coat. "When something is worrying you," he had said, "you can mentally take it off, as if it were a coat, and lay it across Jesus' shoulders. No burden is too great for Him."

"There are no problems too big for God, but a stubborn heart can muffle His voice." Anne's words again. Suddenly Kara realized they were true. "I have been stubborn, haven't I, God?" she whispered. "I should have turned it over to you a long time ago." She thought about her family back at Eagle Lodge.

138

Tia would be in Lariat by now. But the rest of them would be awake. Colin had probably told them that Ryan had drowned, and now she was missing too. She could picture Anne crying and Dad on the radio organizing volunteers and supplies for a search the next day.

"I messed up, Mom," she said aloud. "I should have flagged the helicopter and talked them into searching with an infrared scope." Sheriff Lassen might not have one, but the forest service would.

Another Bible verse popped into her mind. *"If we confess our sins, God is faithful and just and will forgive us our sins and purify us from all unrighteousness."*

Still snug in the sleeping bag, Kara drew up her legs and rested her chin on her knees. Staring out into the beauty of the moonlit forest, she said simply, "I'm sorry, God. If I could take it back, I would, but there's nothing I can do. So please forgive me and watch over Ryan. I know he's out there somewhere. Please keep him safe."

She started singing softly, "Amazing grace, how sweet the sound . . ." By the third verse, she felt drowsy again. She curled up on the lumpy pine mattress, closed her eyes, and fell instantly asleep.

The scream shattered her sleep like an arrow striking glass.

Kara jumped up. Thwack! Her head hit the top of the shelter. She went down again, rubbing the instant lump that had formed on the top of her head and struggling to fight her way out of the sleeping bag.

The scream came again, louder this time, followed by, "Get out of here, you big bully!" Then, "Help! Kara, help meeee!"

Ryan! There was no mistaking her little brother's howl. Kara finally pulled free of the tangled bag. Grateful that she had slept in her clothes, she bolted out of the shelter into the pale, gray light of early morning. Her thick cotton socks did little to save her feet from becoming a pincushion for pinecones and sharp twigs, but Kara hardly noticed as she sped toward Ryan's continued calls for help.

"Leave me alone! Kar-raaa!"

His screams sent chills through her, spurring her on. She started to yell, "I'm coming, Ry," but stopped in time. She would need stealth and a weapon. She came to a halt in front of a huge boulder. Ryan's frantic cries came from the other side. *Please, God,* she prayed silently, *show me what to do!* An instant picture of David preparing to do battle with Goliath flashed through her mind. She nearly laughed out loud, but the message was clear. Quickly, she searched the ground. She needed stones, good-sized ones. She settled for two that she could stuff in her jacket pockets and quickly began to climb the boulder, thankful for stocking feet that kept her approach somewhat quiet. Not that it mattered much. Ryan's clamor continued with the same force as before. Whoever was after him wasn't doing any damage to his voice. And, she realized, it didn't sound as if anyone was hurting him. He sounded as mad as a cornered cat!

At the top of the largest boulder, Kara froze. There below her on the ground were the remains of Ryan's backpack and jacket. It looked like they had been fed through a shredder, with pieces of blue canvas, green nylon, and white cotton padding strewn all over the ground. Heart pounding, her eyes followed the trail of debris across the small clearing to a tall ponderosa pine. She found Ryan about halfway up the trunk, firmly wedged between two stout branches. Eyes squeezed shut and still yelling like crazy, he hung on with one hand while beating at the tree below him with a long, bushy pine frond. At the base of the tree, a large black bear stood on its back legs, clawing the tree trunk, staying just out of reach of Ryan's flimsy weapon.

Kara's chest tightened in fear when she saw the radio collar around the bear's neck. Was it the same animal that attacked Lyman? That ranger, Brad, said it would probably work its way back to its home territory. Was it possible for a bear to travel this far in just a few days?

Kara tried to slow her breathing. So far the animal didn't seem to know she was there. She must be downwind. *"Once they've tasted blood . . ."* The memory of the warning made her stomach churn. *Stay calm.* She couldn't call out—that would scare Ryan, and he might fall out of the tree. She'd give anything for Colin's rifle, but it was back at Eagle Lodge. The only weapons she had were the stones in her pocket.

Okay, God, this time it's all up to You. She hefted a baseball-sized rock from her pocket, drew back, and pitched a hard fastball straight toward the back of the animal's head.

The instant she threw, the bear must have caught the sound of her movement. It turned, and the rock smacked hard into its nose. With a bellow of fury, the animal started toward her, still on two legs, roaring and acting more like a grizzly than a black bear.

Crazy! The minute the thought crossed her mind, Kara knew it had to be true. For whatever reason, this bear was insane. It was capable of anything, and there was no way she could know what it would do next.

"Kara!" Ryan's yell of recognition distracted her for only a moment, but by the time she had snatched up another rock, the creature was already at the base of the boulder. If she didn't give it a good reason to leave, and soon, she was literally dead meat.

"Get him, Kara. Knock him out!"

At Ryan's yell, the bear hesitated and turned back toward the tree. Kara wound up and threw the second stone as hard as she could, aiming for the same spot. It struck just behind a well-padded ear, and the bear turned back to her, huffing loudly, its eyes blazing in fury.

Quickly she scanned the area around her for another weapon. A few larger, heavier rocks were scattered among the stones across the top of her fortress. Instantly, Kara knew what she had to do.

"The Lord is my strength." The same David who killed Goliath had written those words in the Psalms. "Be my strength too, God," she prayed, as she hurried toward one of the bigger rocks. She hefted it into her arms. The weight of it nearly pulled her over as she staggered to the edge of the boulder.

Her appearance sent the bear into another rage. She held her breath and froze in place until the animal was directly below her, then drew air deep into her lungs, lifted the rock as high as she could, and hurtled it straight down. It landed with a crunch right on top of the bear's upturned snout. Blood spattered the rocks and ground as the animal fell. For one heart-stopping moment it swayed on all fours, shaking its head, then, to Kara's relief, it turned and sped off into the woods.

"Whooee! Way to go, Kara!" Ryan had dropped the branch he'd been waving and had both arms locked around the trunk of the tree.

Kara half-jumped, half-slid down the side of the boulder and raced across the clearing. She felt a prickly sensation at the back of her neck, as if the bear was right behind her. One glance proved he wasn't, but that didn't mean he might not return at any moment.

At the base of the tree, she stopped and looked up. "Come on down, Ry, you're safe now."

He shook his head. "I can't. There's no branches to climb on."

He was right. She wanted to ask him how he'd gotten up there, but then she realized adrenaline must have turned him into a monkey. That, or maybe God had given him a push. The tree limbs shifted with his weight when he moved, and she could see him shiver. He was dressed in his sweatshirt and a pair of long johns, with thick wool socks several sizes too big pulled up like leggings over his feet to his knees. The cold morning air called for a jacket.

"Are you hurt anywhere?" When he shook his head no, she breathed a sigh of relief and moved to where he could see her clearly. "Watch me, Ry." She hurried to another tree, sat on the ground, and wrapped both arms and legs around the trunk. "Come down like this. Go slow; I'll stay underneath so you won't fall."

He sniffed and shook his head. The reality of his predicament was sinking in, and Kara was afraid he would stay there all day. That option might keep him safe until the rescue party came, but if that bear came back, it left her as the main course in people stew. Besides, black bears were good climbers and this one was insane, which, in her mind, put them in double jeopardy.

She decided to be truthful and firm. "No choice, Ry. If that bear comes back, we're in real trouble. We've got to get out of here, so do as I say and do it now!"

To her surprise, he drew a shuddering breath, wrapped his body around the trunk, and inched his way to the ground. She guided him the last few feet, then pulled him into a tight hug. "Oh, Ry, I thought we'd lost you!" The last two words came out on a sob, and she clung to him, rubbing his back and smoothing back his hair, just as she'd seen Mom do dozens of times. It was then she knew that with Mom gone, Ryan had become more to her than just a brother; it was like he was her own child.

Ryan squirmed out of her grasp, sniffling, and wiped his nose on the sleeve of his sweatshirt. "Snot-nosed ole bear ate my breakfast, then I thought it was going to eat me, so I climbed the tree."

Kara grinned and brushed away her own tears. "Good thinking, Ry. But let's get out of here, okay? Dad will be coming with a rescue party soon. We need to be closer to the river." She took his hand to lead him back toward the boulders, but he wouldn't budge.

"Wait. I gotta get my stuff!"

Kara studied the remains of Ryan's shredded pack and shook her head. "Sorry, it doesn't look like there's much left."

Ryan frowned. "Not that. My survival kit and bear blanket. Over there." He pointed to a huge, blackened tree stump. The rest of the tree had fallen, struck by lightning, Kara guessed. It had broken at about the halfway mark, and animals, insects, or time had carved a large hole into the base of the trunk. Before she could stop him, Ryan raced toward the stump and returned clutching the canvas pouch he called his survival kit. With his other hand he half dragged, half carried, a large bear hide.

Kara gasped when she realized what he had. "Where did you get that?"

"From Big Foot," Ryan said calmly as he stepped ahead of her. "We'd better go now, Kara, 'cause that bear might come back, and he's gonna be mad."

20

KARA KEPT HER EYES ON the bushes as she pushed Ryan ahead of her. She moved quickly around the boulders and back down the thin trail to the shelter where she had spent the night. The sky had brightened to an eggshell blue, with wisps of white clouds streaking across the tops of the trees.

"Wow, cool!" Ryan crowed when he saw the small pole structure. "I bet Big Foot made this. Yours are pointed at the top."

Kara frowned. "What are you talking about, Ry? There are no Sasquatch around here." She bent down and quickly pulled on her boots. "Besides, no one knows if they're real or not."

Ryan's chin came up, and he pointed to his chest. "I know! Big Foot saved me. He helped me breathe."

Kara stared at him. Was this his imagination? Or had someone really pulled him out of the river? And where did he get that bear hide? "Ry?" She started to ask again where he had found the rug, but the drone of an airplane engine stopped her.

"Yeah! Dad's here! Can we go home now, Kara? 'Cause I'm really hungry."

She smiled and took his hand. "Sure. But we'd better hurry. Walk really fast, but stay with me, okay?"

Quickly Kara led the way back to the river. A few yards from where the raft had tangled with the tree, a rocky beach separated the forest from the river. "If we stand out here," she told Ryan, "they'll see us right away."

The plane had already made one pass, but she knew they'd be back. She watched Ryan struggling to keep the bear hide wrapped around his skinny frame, then took it from him. "Let me see that. Please?" Even without close examination, she could tell the hide had been expertly tanned. She bent down in front of her little brother and said evenly, "Where did you get this, Ry? If you took it from somewhere, I promise you're not in trouble."

Ryan scowled. "I told you! The Sas . . ." Behind her, a branch snapped. Ryan's face turned white, and Kara jumped to her feet. The grunts and huffing sounds coming from the bushes meant only one thing.

Kara dropped the hide and grabbed Ryan's shoulders. "Into the water, quick!" She pushed him ahead of her and waded into the chilly water. It didn't look too deep. If they could make it to the middle of the river, maybe the bear would give up.

Right, Wako. Like bears don't swim. They were nearly halfway across when Ryan put on the brakes.

"I can't! It's slippery. I'm gonna fall!" Tears were coursing down his pale cheeks, and Kara knew he must be really scared. He'd already survived one near drowning. She risked a glance over her shoulder. The bear was on the beach, slapping at the water with his long, black claws. If it charged them in the middle of the river, she had no doubt who would win.

The bear took a step forward into the river, panting and blowing as if it had just run a race. But Kara knew it wasn't exhaustion that made the animal breathe that way—it was

146

excitement. The bear's hunting instinct was in full gear, and they were its prey.

She yanked her pack off her back, swung it around her head three times, and tossed it as hard as she could toward the beach. As she had hoped, it landed behind the animal, distracting it for a minute. Thank God there was still jerky in there. The buzz of an airplane in the distance gave her hope. If they could just make it to the other side of the river . . .

While the bear dug at her pack, she bent her knees and reached behind her for Ryan's arms. "Hurry, Ry, get on my back." The little boy didn't hesitate. With one leap he was on her, arms and legs wrapped tightly around her neck and waist. His weight nearly pitched her into the water. She took a deep breath, stood up straight, and waded deeper into the river. The water came only to her hips, but the current was strong. She slipped twice, nearly losing her footing on the moss-coated rocks.

Then Ryan screamed. Kara spun around, lost her balance, and went to her knees. The swirling water came up to her chin and dragged at her jacket, nearly sweeping her into the current. Ryan kept a death grip on her neck, causing her to choke. She grabbed his hands and pulled them off her throat enough so that she could breathe. Not that she could get much air. The bear had waded into the river. It stood on all four feet, belly deep, watching them from about four feet away. Beads of water clung to its cinnamon-colored coat, and sunshine glinted off the radio collar around its neck. If the animal had not been stalking them it would have made a neat picture.

This is definitely not a Kodak moment! The silly thought spurred Kara to action. She stood and backed slowly toward the opposite bank. The bear kept pace with her, as if they were playing a game of Mother-May-I, but Kara knew this

147

wasn't a game. *Please, God,* she prayed, *don't let me fall!* If she so much as stumbled, they were dead meat!

"Freeze!" The shout stopped her in her tracks. "Wakara, stand still!"

Kara did as she was told. The boom of a rifle shattered the air as a bullet whizzed over the bear's rump, just grazing the fur. The animal spun around, and with amazing speed disappeared into the brush. The next thing Kara knew, Colin was at her elbow, prying Ryan's arms from the chokehold around her neck. He hefted the boy over one shoulder and grabbed Kara's arm. "Come on, let's get out of here."

Colin's grip on her arm kept her upright as they struggled through the swift-flowing current into calmer water, then finally onto the rock-strewn shore. When Colin released her, she went to her knees, shaking from cold and fatigue. Ryan was shivering, his teeth chattering, his skin pale. She pulled him into her arms and began rubbing him down with her hands. There was nothing else to work with. Her pack was gone, and every scrap of her clothing was soaking wet.

"I w-wish I had my b-b-bear blanket!" He looked longingly across the river at the patch of brown fur lying on the sand.

"I wish you did too, Ry." Kara rubbed harder, chafing his arms and legs as if she were trying to start a fire.

"Ow, Kara, not so hard!" He squirmed out of her grasp, and she was relieved to see his face had regained some color.

Colin was speaking into a walkie-talkie, radioing in their position. Kara took a deep breath and scrambled to her feet. "Dad will be here soon." She said it to reassure herself as much as Ryan. The boy nodded and took a step toward Colin.

It was then Kara saw the bear. It must have crossed the river—circled around them. Her mouth went dry, and she called out a warning, but it was too late.

148

The animal charged straight at Colin, knocking him down. The walkie-talkie flew out of his hands and landed with a splash in the river, while the rifle spun along the ground, coming to rest just out of reach of Colin's grasping hands.

Kara screamed, "Ryan, run!" She pushed him behind her and made a dive for the gun.

Colin had rolled onto his belly and folded both hands behind his head, protecting his neck. The bear tore at Colin's backpack, shredding the nylon and popping the zipper with one swipe of its paw. Kara scrambled to her knees and fired. The shot passed harmlessly over the animal's back and struck with a solid thud into the trunk of a tree. Scraps of bark flew in all directions, but the bear didn't even look up.

Colin screamed as the bear's claws made contact with his shoulder, slicing through his denim jacket like a knife through butter. Kara's hands were shaking. She jumped to her feet, drew in a deep breath, and took careful aim. She couldn't miss. Not this time. If she did, Colin was dead, and most likely so was she.

A shot rang out. With a howl of pain and rage, the bear rose to its hind feet, blood pouring from a wound in its shoulder. Kara's heart thudded in fear as the animal took two steps toward her. Then she heard shouts and the sound of heavy boots crashing through the brush, accompanied by the clatter of helicopter blades directly overhead. The bear kept coming, but ran right past her into the bushes on the far side of the clearing.

Ryan raced into her line of vision. He stopped a few feet from Colin and began jumping up and down. "They're here, they're here. It's okay, Colin, you can get up now. That ole bear is history!"

Before she could react, two rangers ran into the clearing. One went directly to Colin, then began talking into his radio. The other took her arm and led her to a fallen log. "Here, young lady, sit down. Put your head between your knees."

She wanted to laugh and tell him she wasn't going to faint, but tiny bursts of light were popping in front of her eyes, and she knew she was about to lose it. She lowered her head and took a deep breath as the wave of dizziness passed. A hand massaged her neck, while another took her pulse.

"Good girl. Take it easy, now. Are you hurt?"

She managed to shake her head. "No, I'm fine. It's Colin."

The hand on her neck shifted to her back. "It's okay, we're on it. He's going to be fine."

She raised her head just as two more rangers strode onto the rocky beach carrying a stretcher. She recognized Brad as the one bending over Colin, and then Dad was there. He scooped up Ryan and hurried over to her, bending down, lifting her chin, and stroking her hair. "Wakara, are you all right?"

"She's okay, Dad." Ryan's voice squeaked with excitement. "Did you see that? Kara shot that ole bear. She got him good."

Kara stared at the rifle, still lying where she'd dropped it on the sand. Then it hit her. "Dad?"

"What is it, Sugar Bear?"

"It wasn't me. I never fired a second shot."

21

THE CHOPPER LIFTED COLIN and two paramedics to safety, while the rangers went after the bear. Dad stripped off Ryan's wet clothes, then took off his own jacket and zipped it around the boy. The warm coat reached nearly to Ryan's ankles, and Kara was relieved to see he had stopped shivering. One of the men had given her a blanket. Dad held it for her while she turned her back, stripped off her soggy sweatshirt, then wrapped the scratchy wool tightly around her shoulders. It wasn't perfect, but it would have to do.

"Mark probably turned back to land at the mill sight," Dad said. "He'll fly us back to Eagle Lodge from there, while Greg takes the horses."

Kara's head snapped up. "You brought Lily?"

Dad nodded. "Colin, Greg, and I rode in, just in case there was nowhere to land a helicopter."

Kara nodded, and in spite of her exhaustion, quickened her pace. Five minutes later, she heard Lily's shrill whinny. "Coming, girl!" Kara laughed and raced to where Greg had the horses tied to trees in a small clearing. She tried to talk Dad into letting her ride all the way to Eagle Lodge, but when they got to the mill sight, he insisted she and Ryan get into the plane with him. "No argument, young lady. You and your brother are wet and cold. I want you back at the lodge as fast as possible."

Kara knew he was right. Almost before they left the ground, Ryan dropped off to sleep with his head on Dad's shoulder. She knew Dad was anxious to hear what had happened, and she was anxious to explain, but she was in the front with Mark, and the drone of the single-engine plane made it hard to talk. In minutes, she caught sight of Eagle Lodge and felt a flood of relief. She had some apologizing to do, but it was sure good to be home.

Her blue sweats, a roaring fire, and a belly full of Anne's hot chicken soup were almost enough to make Kara forget the ordeal of the past two days. But Ryan was awake and chattering a mile a minute. Dad finally hushed him. "Slow down, Tiger, you're not making any sense." He sat down next to the hearth, facing both of them. Anne had settled in one of the comfortable chairs, while Greg pulled a straight-backed chair closer to the fire.

"Okay," Dad began, "Colin told us what happened with the raft." He looked at Kara. "He takes the blame for that, by the way. And for leaving you behind." Kara winced. Dad's look told her that he didn't for a minute believe that last part. He knew her too well.

Dad's gaze shifted to Ryan. "What I want to know now is what happened afterward."

"My turn?" Ryan sounded so eager, and Kara almost laughed at the excitement gleaming in those huge, brown eyes. Dad nodded. "What happened when you fell into the river, Son? How did you get to shore?"

Ryan frowned. "I don't remember. I think Big Foot got me out. I was coughing, then he turned me upside down, then I threw up and he took me to his log cabin. It's so cool! Lots of animals all over the walls, and bear furs, like the blanket he gaved me." He glared at Kara. "Kara don't believe me, but it's true."

He turned back to Dad. "He made me put on dry clothes and cooked me some stew, then he gave me the bear blanket and told me to go to sleep. When I woke up it was dark, and he wrapped me in the blanket and carried me into the woods. I was scared until I heard Kara singing, but Big Foot said we should play a game. He tol' me to crawl into the hollow log with my pack and blanket and count to one hundred, then I could go surprise Kara. But when I started counting, he went away to hide. I must have fell asleep, because then it was a little light outside and that snotty ole bear was sniffing my legs." He stopped to catch his breath.

"I thought that stupid bear was gonna' eat me, so I kicked it in the nose and threw my pack at him and climbed the tree. Then I started screamin', and Kara came and chased the bear away." He grinned. "She got him good, but he wouldn't leave us alone, then Colin came and the bear jumped on him."

Kara's thoughts echoed the puzzled look on Dad's face. Ryan wouldn't make up a cabin with animal trophies and hides. And he wasn't wearing his own clothes when she found him, Kara suddenly remembered.

Before she could say anything, the screen door banged, and Brad walked in carrying what was left of her backpack and the bear hide they had abandoned on the beach. He joined them in the dining room and accepted a cup of coffee from Anne while he listened to Dad's version of Ryan's adventure. Instead of sharing their confusion, Brad just nodded and said, "That's about what we suspected." He grinned at Ryan. "Your Big Foot's name is Charlie Fox. He's lived in the woods up that way for a couple of years now. We've seen his cabin, and we know he's poaching animal hides and meat, but we haven't ever caught him in the act."

Brad turned to Kara. "It was Charlie's shot that wounded the bear, by the way. We picked him up at his cabin about an hour later. He was gathering up hides, getting ready to take off. I doubt we have enough evidence to convict him, though. This time he shot an animal to save someone's life." Brad smiled at Kara. "Can't call that poaching, can we?"

Kara shook her head. "No, I guess not." She glanced over at Greg, then turned back to Brad. "Uh, about the bear. It had a radio collar. Was it the same bear that attacked Lyman?"

Brad sighed. "I'm afraid so." He turned to Dad. "I told you relocation doesn't always work."

Dad's mouth was quivering as he stared hard at Ryan. "Looks like Charlie Fox saved more than one life in the last couple of days." He turned to Brad. "Please tell him I'm grateful."

Brad nodded, "I will if I see him." He handed Ryan the bear rug. "Here you go. Charlie said he wanted you to keep this."

After Brad left, Anne went into the kitchen to fix a real meal, and Greg got on the radio to see if he could get reports on Colin and Tia. When Ryan yawned and snuggled into his "bear blanket," Dad motioned to Kara and led her into the rec room, where a smaller fire was burning in the other fireplace. The hall door was propped open so heat could flow to the other rooms. "This is fine," he said. He pointed her to a sling-back canvas chair beside the hearth, while he leaned with his back against the pool table.

Here we go, she thought, *it's lecture time.* "Dad," she began, wanting to explain why she had stayed behind and hidden from the search helicopter, but instead of letting her continue, he held up his hand.

"Wait, Wakara, please. I want to hear your story, but I need to say a couple of things first." He cleared his throat, and she could see tears welling up in his eyes. "I have to

154

tell you, I was angry when Colin confessed his responsibility for the accident—angry at him, and at you for being so stubborn about coming home. But now I realize that if you hadn't stayed, that bear could very well have gotten to Ryan, and we might have lost him anyway. I . . . I'm glad you were there, Sugar Bear. I just hope none of you give us quite this big of a scare again." He shook his head, then his mouth twitched in a smile. "Unless you're trying to drive your old man into a rest home before he turns fifty, do you think we can do without any more great adventures for a while?"

Kara sat there stunned. Dad wasn't mad at her. He wasn't even blaming her for any of this. She sighed in relief. "I'll try, Dad. It's not like I wanted any of it to happen." She scowled and rubbed out a spark from the fire that had landed on the hearth by her feet. "I can't believe Colin made such a selfish, stupid decision. And he called me an idiot for not getting back in the raft." Tears of frustration made her eyes burn. "He wrote Ryan off, Dad, right away. Like there was no chance he might be alive. When I saw the life jacket on shore, I knew Ryan had made it, but Colin wouldn't listen. All he could talk about was bringing in divers."

The more she talked, the tighter her chest got. She had to stop and force air into her lungs, then let it out on a heavy sigh. "I mean, I'm sorry Colin got hurt, and I hope he's okay, but he was wrong, Dad. Wrong about everything. And I was wrong about him. How could I have ever thought we might have a future together?"

When she realized what she had said, she clamped a hand over her mouth, but Dad was still leaning on the pool table, listening with a patient expression on his face. If he was shocked by her feelings for Colin, or rather her past feelings for Colin, he didn't show it. And he didn't look angry anymore either—just sad.

155

When she didn't say anything else, Dad stepped toward her and pulled her up into a hug. When he released her, he held onto her shoulders and looked into her eyes. "Do me one favor, Sugar Bear?" She nodded, and he smiled softly. "Do some research in your Bible on forgiveness, then get Colin's side of the story before you write him off the same way you think he did your little brother."

22

"WAKARA! I THOUGHT YOU'D NEVER get home!" Tia sat up cross-legged on her bed. "It's so boring around here, and Doc Glenn says I can't ride for six weeks!" She groaned and leaned back on her pillows. "There goes rodeo season for this entire year!"

Kara pulled the desk chair closer to the bed. "I'm sorry." She squeezed her friend's hand. "I wish this hadn't happened, but like my dad keeps reminding me, we can't go back, we have to go forward." She cleared her throat and fought back another surge of anger. It seemed like all she'd done the past three days was cry or steam. She was still so mad at Colin she could spit!

To distract herself, Kara leaned over to the bedside table and smelled a lavender rosebud, one of six in a clear glass vase. "Where'd you get the flowers? They're gorgeous!"

Tia grinned. "Colin. He's been over twice since he got out of the hospital. I guess he feels like it's his fault or something."

"No kidding." Kara quickly set the vase back on the table. She wanted to change the subject, but Tia was watching her like a cat at a mouse hole.

"Come on, Wakara, can't you cut him some slack? He feels really bad, you know. Like we all died or something. But we didn't." She shrugged. "Hey, stuff happens. Anyway, you should see his shoulder! The stitches look like railroad tracks. The doc said he's lucky the bear didn't rip up any muscles or anything."

Kara's stomach felt queasy. "Can't we talk about something else?"

Tia shrugged. "Sure." She picked at the blue fuzz on her blanket. "But I wouldn't be your friend if I didn't tell you Colin is really beating himself up inside. Like, he doesn't understand why you won't talk to him." She lowered her voice. "He's talking about going away, Wakara. And I think, if you let him do that, you'll be really sorry."

"You and Dad." Kara swallowed the lump in her throat. "Colin's not home right now." She knew it was no excuse—she'd had plenty of time to see Colin after the accident, but she just couldn't face him yet, her feelings were too mixed up. "He went back to Eagle Lodge to help Greg," she went on. "They're bringing Lyman home today, and the vet told them to stop every ten minutes to let him rest."

Tia shrugged. "What did you bring me?" She pointed to the book Kara had laid on the table next to the roses.

Glad for a change of subject, Kara snagged the blue binder. "Great-grandpa Harley's journal."

"Hey, cool!" Tia sat up straighter. "Where'd we leave off?"

"Right here where Irish is talking about Kathleen. She must have been his first wife or his fiancée, remember? She died and he was really upset." Kara flipped to the page she had marked with a yellow sticky tab. "Then it skips to August 1, 1907." She began to read.

Arrived in Sacramento end of July.
The heat is stifling. We've stocked up on
supplies and are headed out tomorrow.

Kara frowned and turned the page. "There aren't any more entries until December. He talks about the cold weather and how they had to come back to the city."

The claim didn't pan out as well as we would like. I managed to find a room over Murphy's, an establishment that passes as a Pub, and not in the best part of town. I must admit that for the first time since my Kathleen died, I'm feeling a bit homesick.

"Poor guy," Tia sympathized. Kara nodded and went on reading.

I'm sweeping floors and washing dishes, but Clemens has taken to the poker table again. He says he will earn us a stake for another try at the gold fields this spring. I believe he cheats and hope he doesn't wind up dead.

"Whoa, listen to this, Tia. It's not dated, but it can't be too much later, because he talks about a huge ice storm."

I feel I may go crazy staring at four dirty walls night and day. Clemens has won himself a wife—an Indian woman, real quiet and shy. I told him

159

what I thought about his heathen ways.
He didn't much like it.

"Wow!" Tia was leaning over the book, trying to read upside down. Kara shifted onto the bed and settled next to her, leaning back against the pillows. "There aren't any more entries in the journal, but Grandpa Sheridan found this along with everything else in that old trunk." She pulled a sealed envelope from the back of the book and handed it to Tia. "Here, you read it. I'm too nervous."

Tia opened the envelope. "Whoa. This was torn out of the journal too. Listen."

Clemens has turned mean. The Indian woman is over forty and is with child. Clemens has threatened to kill both her and the man who lost her in a game of cards. I have terminated my association with the scoundrel, but am not as yet able to depart for home. A lack of funds keeps me here. That, and my fear for the safety of the woman and her unborn child.

Tia took a deep breath. "Oh, Wakara, this is awful! But do you see what this means?"

Kara just nodded. She couldn't talk around the lump in her throat. Tia squeezed her hand. "Want to stop?" Kara shook her head no, and Tia scanned the rest of the page. "Boy, it really skips ahead." She continued reading.

The child was born last night. Clemens left the Pub with a shotgun. I am

troubled, and feel I must see to the
welfare of this poor woman and her
child, though I don't really know what I
can do except to pray.

"This part is really scribbled," Tia frowned, "and the sentences are weird."

Followed into the woods, but unarmed
and too far away. One shot. Too late.
"Wakara," she says, and hands me the
babe. The woman was dead, I swear I
wouldn't have left her otherwise. Had
to run—Clemens insane. God forgive me
for not acting in a more timely
manner.

Tia unfolded the second page and gasped. "Oh, look. It's a letter to Wakara! Your great-grandmother." She dropped the sheet into Kara's lap. "You'd better read it." Kara picked it up and stared at the neat, clear handwriting. She swallowed back tears and began to read.

My dear Wakara,
I am amazed at the goodness of God. For me, these past
sixteen years have been an agony of waiting, but I do not
regret a moment of it. I hope you understand that I could
not keep you with me. A man alone with a baby is sure
to come under suspicion—I had trouble enough on the
train from California to Oregon. Finding the Hilyard's was
a miracle. That they were missionaries and willing to
adopt you was an even greater miracle. Each time I
visited I intended it to be my last, as you were in good
hands and did not need me, but I could not stay away.

Now that you have agreed to marry me and we have your parents' blessing, I am indeed the happiest man alive. I am forever yours,

Harley W. Sheridan

Kara took a deep breath and closed her eyes. She could picture Irish, thirty-eight years old and deeply in love with his beautiful Indian bride. She thought about the girl in her great-grandfather's drawing. They had only a few years together. He must have been devastated when she died.

"It all makes sense now, Tia." Kara sat up and wiped the tears from her eyes. "My Great-grandmother Wakara could easily have had some Yahi blood. Her mother lived in Sacramento. Anne said some of the Yahi people escaped the massacre and were taken into other tribes."

Tia sighed. "You're right. And who knows?" she said dreamily. "Your great-grandmother could have been related to Ishi—the Yahi Indian they found starving to death in California."

Kara smiled and rolled her eyes. "Not likely."

Tia flashed her an indignant look. "Why not? It was Ishi's mother who had the nickname, Wakara."

Kara sighed. "Well, as Mrs. Kroeber said in her book, Ishi was the last of his tribe, and he died in 1916, so I guess we'll never know."

A horn honked in the driveway, and Mrs. Sanchez called up the stairs, "Wakara, your father's here."

Dad moved over and let her take the wheel, and Kara concentrated on her driving. When they pulled into the driveway, Dad got out of the car and pointed to the bunkhouse. "Colin's home. He and Greg got in half an hour ago."

"Thanks, Dad." Kara was determined not to get into another conversation about Colin. She parked the car down by the barn and went in to check Lyman. He was standing quietly munching hay. As far as she could tell, none of the wounds had broken open. An empty syringe in the tack room trash can told her Greg had given his horse a dose of Banamine. Good. Lyman was bound to be sore after the trip up Pine Creek Trail. She rubbed between his ears, gave him an apple treat, and went into the next stall to pet Lily. All the horses had been fed and watered. She gave them all a treat, then closed up the barn and hurried into the house.

Anne already had dinner on the table, and Kara pushed back a wave of disappointment when Greg came in alone. *I will not stress over Colin Jones,* she told herself as she reached for the bowl of mashed potatoes.

"Where's Colin?" Ryan broke the silence. "I wanted to show him my new John Wayne movie. Mark gave it to me as a present for almost being drowned."

Greg shook his head. "I wouldn't count on it. Colin went into town for pizza. He said not to wait up for him."

Dad frowned. "That doesn't sound like Colin; he always eats with the family. Although I guess his time off is his own." He glanced at Kara, and she felt herself blush.

"What?" she said. "It's not my fault if Colin has decided he likes pizza better than Anne's cooking." Greg and Dad just looked at her. She tried to ignore them and finish her dinner, but the roast beef tasted like rawhide, and the mashed potatoes turned to mush in her mouth.

When everyone had finished, she helped Anne clean up the kitchen. As she put the last of the silverware into the dishwasher, Greg burst into the room. "Where's Dad?" He was out of breath, and the ashen color of his face made Kara's stomach knot.

"What's wrong?" But the minute she asked him, she knew.

"Colin's gone. He left a note saying he felt that under the circumstances, it would be best for all of us if he left the Sheridans' employ."

Anne moaned and sat down on the nearest chair. Kara stared at Greg. "Gone? What do you mean, gone? That note doesn't sound like Colin at all!"

Greg stared back at her, a hard look on his face. "You're right, it doesn't. But then, Colin hasn't been himself since the accident. He can't forgive himself for making what he calls 'a stupid mistake,' and some of us haven't made it any easier on him."

Kara felt stunned. Could Colin really be gone? Worse, could she have driven him away? Greg broke into her thoughts. "Tell Dad I'm going after him, and I *will* bring him back." He snagged his jacket and hat off the rack on the service porch and let the back door slam behind him.

As the pickup truck rattled down the drive, Kara's thoughts raged—*Colin can't be gone, he's part of the family— But he betrayed us because he wanted a thrill, and it almost got Ryan killed—Everyone makes mistakes—That was more than a mistake, it was a deliberate choice.*

The knot in Kara's stomach tightened until it was hard to draw a breath. She sat down heavily at the kitchen table and felt Anne's hand cover her own. When she looked up, she realized Dad had come back into the kitchen.

"I heard," he said, and joined them at the table. "Don't worry, Greg will find Colin, and when he does, we'll settle this once and for all." Anne nodded, moved over to the sink, and began making a fresh pot of coffee. Dad turned to Kara. "Take my advice and talk to him, Wakara. Don't bury your anger. Believe me, it only makes things worse."

Anne spoke up. "Anger hides in darkness, but the devil cannot get at what is in the light."

"You're both telling me to forgive him, right?" Kara's hands were shaking, and she folded them in her lap. "What if I can't? Sure, he admits he made a stupid mistake, but his mistake could have cost Ryan his life."

"Have you never made a mistake?" Dad asked softly.

"Well, sure, but not one that serious."

"All have sinned," Anne reminded her quietly. "Our sins cost Jesus His life."

Kara sat there stunned. "Oh." She couldn't think of anything else to say. *"Forgiving each other, just as in Christ God forgave you."* Her cheeks were wet with tears, but she didn't rub them away. Jesus had forgiven her. He'd forgiven Colin too. What right did she have to say Colin's sins were worse than hers were?

The knot in Kara's stomach loosened. She felt quiet inside. *Please, God, bring Colin home,* she prayed silently. *I'll make it right, I promise.* Anne was pouring coffee into mugs, and Dad got up to help her. Kara sat still, enjoying the feeling of peace, like snuggling under the covers on a stormy night.

Dad and Anne joined her at the table. She wrapped her fingers around the coffee mug and realized her hands had stopped shaking. When she heard the sound of tires on gravel, a thrill of hope shot through her. "They're home!" She jumped to her feet and raced to the window. The truck came to a stop in front of the bunkhouse. In the glow of the halogen light, she could see two people in the cab. She ran to the back door, but before she jerked it open, she turned around. "Thanks, Dad; thanks, Anne. I owe you one."

Dad gave her a thumbs up, and Anne flashed her an understanding smile.

Linda Shands is a prolific writer of magazine articles and the author of four adult novels and one nonfiction book. She loves the Oregon wilderness and lives in the small town of Cottage Grove with her husband, a cat, two horses, and twin golden retrievers.

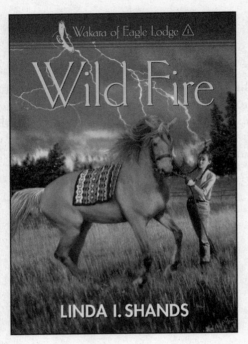

Blind Fury

Wakara learns more about being a child of God but struggles to trust Him. When her dad and brother get lost in a snowstorm, Wakara has to think fast and pray hard to try to save them—and herself.

0-8007-5747-5